THE BLOOD KING

JORDAN BENSON

Contents

1

CHAPTER 1

"The Blood King was the most ruthless king Thesonia has ever seen. He killed thousands, he took no prisoners, and he conquered everyone who stood in his way," Ms. McIntire said dramatically, pacing back and forth across the front of the classroom. "If our brave hero Galen Rivero didn't slay him, it's safe to say the he could have taken over all of Europe and possibly the world!"

Cora found it hard to believe that just one man that lived thousands of years ago was capable of taking over all of Europe, much less the world. Cora always believed her history teachers had a tendency to stretch the truth, but none of her classmates seem to question it so neither would she.

Cora's thoughts drifted off until the bell rang.

She immediately jumped up out of her seat before any of her classmates had time to respond and bolted out the door.

Finally, high school was over. She was free. It was a wonderful feeling she felt as she skipped through the halls waving her arms around like a lunatic, which caught a lot of stares from teachers scattered throughout the halls. Nothing could dampen her mood today.

As she stepped outside she was welcomed by the rays of the sun smiling down on her.

Shortly after, her father came to pick her up. She greeted him with a warm embrace like she always did, being carful not to crush his injured spine.

"I'm so proud of you, sweetheart! I never thought I'd see the day Coraline 'I'm too cool for school' Bowman actually finished high school," he teased.

Cora was slightly annoyed but, in her mind nothing could ruin this day.

In the backseat of the car she found cupcakes that spelled out "Congratulations Cora!" Undoubtedly her grandmother's doing.

As was Thessionian tradition, today Cora was officially considered an adult. Cora's father brought her to the resting grounds, which are a Thessonian cemetery of sorts. Thanks to Thessoinian crystals, the bodies of loved ones can be preserved for several millennia.

As Cora and her father entered the resting grounds, Cora spotted a familiar face.

"Dimitri!" She squealed and ran up to the young man, nearly tackling him.

"Cora!" he says with huge smile on his face. "Guess what I got today?" he asked, running his fingers through his tight, black curls.

Cora placed a hand on her chin pondering his question.

"This!" He pulled a sword out of his sheath.

The sword truly is breathtaking. It's made of black steel and decorated with amethysts. It matched perfectly with his dark leather pants and belt and his dark purple trench coat he always wore.

Cora couldn't help but be envious of her best friend. They had known each other for as long as she could remember. Their fathers were warriors in the same guild, they fought side by side until her father's injury. Their entire lives, Cora and Dimitri had wanted to be warriors just like them.

"Do you like it?" Dimitri asked.

"It's the most beautiful sword I've ever seen!"

She exclaimed.

"Dimitri, lets go!" His twin sister Scarlet called out. Even in this heat her dark bronze skin and wavy hair look as flawless as ever.

Cora and Dimitri split up and visited their respective relatives.

Cora kneeled beside the lifeless bodies of her ancestors. She came from a long line of warriors on her fathers side.

"I will make you proud." she whispered before leaving.

She arrived at home to find her mother preparing dinner.

"How was your last day of school?" Mother asked.

"Same old." Cora responded. "I saw Dimitri at the resting grounds today and he had the coolest sword!"

"Don't tell me you're still pursuing this warrior dream of yours," her mother interrupted not looking up from the counter.

"As a matter of fact I am, Mom, I've been practicing all the time," the young girl argued

"So did your father, and look where it got him!" Her mother exclaimed angrily.

"Let the girl dream, Karen," her grandmother said looking up from her book.

"I'm gonna go," Coraline said as she exited the room.

Later that night, while the rest of her family was asleep, young Cora was about to do something that was going to alter the course of her life.

My whole family were warriors, she thought to her self. If mom won't let me have my own sword I'm sure no one would mind if a I borrowed one. They're all dead anyways, she thought.

She searched through her grandmother's study. She had never really been in here before.

The room was so dark, it was nearly impossible to see anything. She felt along the wall for a light switch. As she felt near the fireplace she felt a small lever and out of pure curiosity she pulled it down.

All of a sudden the fireplace, disappeared and a passage way opened up. All she could see way a red glowing light at the end of the passage.

It's felt like she was in a trance, all she knew how to do was keep walking towards the light like a moth to a flame.

When she reached the end she was shocked by what she saw.

A boy not much older the her completely frozen in crystal just like the dead in the resting grounds, but instead of looking peaceful he looked like he was in anguish desperate to escape this prison. The boy had black hair, that went down to his knees. He wore a red cape the color of blood.

His clothes were as black as his hair all except for one leg that appeared to be made of metal.

The look in his red eyes made her shiver. "Who is he?" She asked herself. She didn't want to know.

"I need to get out of here," she said to herself.

Then as she turned towards the exit something glimmering caught her eye. The blade was black as night and the diamonds and rubies encrusted in it sparkled like the stars. No, it put the stars to shame. It was right within her grasp and she grabbed it.

It was stuck. She pulled harder and harder again and again until it finally broke free.

She took the sword and ran out of the passage, carefully shutting it after she left.

What she didn't notice was that the crystal prison holding the young man began to crumble away.

2

— • —

CHAPTER 2

The Sorting Day is the day where every young Thessionian between the ages of 17-20 competes in a series of challenges to see what career they will be assigned to. The top 50% get into the Prestige Program and become very successful. The bottom 50% usually work in sanitation, factories or fixing things. You may attempt to get into the Prestige Program as many times as you want.

No matter how hard she tried she couldn't sleep. If she was ever going to become a great warrior she would need to get into the Prestige Program and soon.

Her eyes drifted to the stolen sword lying on her desk. Just looking at it made her feel uneasy. She couldn't shake the feeling she had made a mistake. Maybe I should put it back. She thought to herself. No, she couldn't, surely all of her competitors would have swords of their own.

She couldn't stop thinking about the boy. No matter how hard she tried she couldn't get his cold red eyes out of her mind. Who is he? Why is he here and not at the resting grounds? Does anyone else know he's here? Should I tell someone? These were all questions running through Cora's mind.

As the sun rose Cora quickly got dressed and then heard a knock on the door.

She quickly hid the sword under her bed. "Come in!"she yelled.

Her father entered the room with one hand behind his back followed by her grandmother. "Good morning, sunshine. How did you sleep?" Her grandmother asked.

"Like a baby," the blonde lied.

"We've got got a little something for your big day." Her father said removing his hand from behind his back to reveal he was holding a sword.

Her blue eyes lit up with excitement. As she closely examined the sword. It was a light silver color with turquoise jewels. It had a blue handle with the face of a lion at the end, her favorite animal.

She threw her arms around and hugged him tighter than she can recall ever hugging anyone, nearly forgetting about his injured back. She eventually let go and proceeded to hug her grandmother.

"I love it but, what will Mom say?" she questioned.

"I'll talk to her," the girl's father responded. "You just focus on doing your best."

"I will," But she couldn't focus. All she could do was think about the boy and the sword and the passage until she arrived at the building where The Sorting was going to take place.

The building was swarmed with people roughly her age. It was so loud she could barely hear herself think. It was so overwhelming, all she could do was stand with her mouth open, staring at all the commotion.

She overheard several conversations. "Did you hear about Prince Lyon?"... "Is it true he's really here? ... "I wonder what he's like in real life."

A tap on her shoulder brought her back to reality. She turned around to see a woman about half her height holding a clipboard.

"Name?" the woman asked tiredly.

"Coraline Bowman."

"What's your address?"

"127 Seaview street."

"Come with me."

Cora followed the woman into a small office.

"Have a seat, let's not waste anytime," the woman said. "If you make it into the Prestige Program what class do you plan on taking technology, politics, or..."

"I want to be a warrior." Cora interrupted.

"That's an honorable aspiration," The woman said. "Your parents must be very proud."

The young girl said nothing. She couldn't help but think of her mother's words

The woman stuck something to the back of Cora's sweatshirt. Upon further inspection Cora discovered it was a target.

The woman shook her head and let out a deep sigh. "Good luck, kid." She said as she escorted the girl out of the office.

Cora was on her way from the office to the main hall where the rest of the competitors were, when she saw a strange looking shadow. She blinked and it was gone. She pushed the thought aside as a figment of her imagination, a side effect of sleep deprivation, until she felt hands grab on to her. She tried to scream but, the stranger placed his hand over her mouth. He came too close for comfort, put his sword on her throat, and whispered in her ear.

"Here's how this is gonna go, you're gonna tell me everything you know about the Blood King and if you scream, I'll kill you."

"I don't know what you're talking about." She said gasping for air.

He threw her face down on the ground and her nose began to bleed.

"Don't play dumb with me!" he yelled.

She reached into her sheath and pulled out her sword and blocked his incoming blow. He attempts another swing but she barely dodged it. On his third strike he finally landed a hit on her arm. She winced in pain but, she knew she couldn't stop fighting. She seized the moment and knocked the sword out of his hand. But to her dismay, he pulled out two more swords from his sleeves.

He began to slowly walk towards her. She ran faster than she'd ever run in her life through the hallways, never once looking back to see how far behind he was until she was back in the main hall with the competitors. She nearly collapsed on the couch still barely able to breathe. Her vision was blurry.

"Are you all right?" she heard an unfamiliar voice ask her.

"Yes. Maybe. I don't know," was all she could respond.

"Is there anything I can do for you?" the voice asked.

"No."she responded politely.

"Well, if you think of anything your wish is my command," He said as Cora's eyes shifted back into focus. Standing in front of her was a tall, well built man, undoubtedly a few years older than her. His skin didn't have a single mark or blemish. His eyes were like sparkling emeralds and he had long scarlet hair that went far past his waist. His clothes looked as if it would take a year's wages to be able to afford them.

Even though Cora was never really interested in the royal family, she still recognized him right away. "You're Prince Lyon!" she exclaimed.

"You are very observant," He said, glancing down at his heart shaped ring. "Tell me, how did you figure it out?"

The Thessionian royal family is very private and hardly ever makes public appearances and has a strict ban on photographs.

"It's your hair. Thessionian kings are supposed to really long hair right?"

"Yes, it was believed by the kings of the past that it would give you strength like Samson. It's mostly just tradition now," he said.

Cora was about to speak, but she was interrupted by a group of girls in matching white armor. They all curtsey before Prince Lyon, then one of them spoke.

"Greetings, your majesty. I haven't seen you since the charity gala," she said.

Prince Lyon stared at the girl for a few moments raising his eyebrows slightly trying to identify her. "You're Governor Martinez' daughter aren't you?"

"Adriana," she corrected seeming slightly offended.

"I heard the White Diamonds were ranked as one of the best high school guilds in southern Thessionia," he said.

"We've been in the top ten high school guilds for the past five years," she replied.

"How is your sister?" he asked looking around the room.

"Same old Val, you shouldn't concern yourself with her," she said inching closer to him.

Cora just sat in silence trying to wrap her head around that fact that she was attacked by a shadow and now she's meeting the prince this was too much for her to handle.

Then all of a sudden a voice came through the loudspeakers. "We regret to inform you that instead of our usual half, the

Prestige Program will only be excepting the top 25%. Thank you for your cooperation."

Those words made Cora's heart sink. She had no idea what she was going to do now.

3

CHAPTER 3

"How could I be so stupid?" she asked herself. "I just talked to the prince and I didn't even bow. Are you supposed to bow? I don't know." Her thoughts were interrupted by the sound of someone calling her name.

"Cora!" She turned around to see Dimitri walking towards her.

She ran towards her best friend meeting him halfway across the hall. "It's so nice to see a familiar face," she said wearily.

"Is everything okay?" he asked.

"It's been a crazy day," she replied.

Coraline just noticed that Scarlet was standing behind him. Cora and Dimitri had been best friends forever but Cora and Scarlet never really hit it off. They used to play together when they were very young but they just always seemed to be in separate worlds.

Cora caught a glimpse of Scarlet staring at one of the other competitors. A boy with short, spiky, auburn hair wearing some sort of steampunk googles on the top of his head. His face was splattered with freckles and his smile was crooked but charming.

"Do you know him?" Cora asked Scarlet.

"No, he just asked me to make an alliance with him," she answered.

"What did you say?" Dimitri asked.

"No," she said with a look of disgust on her face. "He wouldn't stop talking about how great of a warrior our father is. He's just a factory worker trying to use my skills to get through."

Several people believed that non-Prestige people were untrustworthy but Cora had no reason to believe that he was using Scarlet.

"I'm sure he didn't mean it like that." Cora said.

Scarlet shook her head. "You are far too trusting Cora. Someone is going to take advantage of that."

Cora was unsure what to make out of that advice when a man holding a bunch of papers stepped up on the podium.

"May I have your attention please. The rules will only be explained once so I suggest you pay attention." He said with a scowl. "Since there are roughly 400 of you competing today this is how we've decided to sort you. As you can see you all have literal targets on your backs. To pass you must eliminate 3 other players. To eliminate another player you must hit there target 3 times. If your targets been hit 3 times you're out."

Then a loud voice came over the loudspeakers. "Thank you for your cooperation. May the Sorting begin."

The platform beneath their feet rose up carrying them up to an enormous arena.

Everyone's targets lit up and people immediately began to attack to try to take out each-others target.

Cora ran and hid behind a brick wall going over the rules in her head...you have to take out 3 opponents, you get 3 strikes you're out.

Cora heard incoherent muttering coming from around the corner saying something about the online order portal gun being a scam and he'd have to use something else to pass. Cora saw this as her chance to launch a sneak attack. She crept as quietly as she possibly could, but when she tried to attack, her opponent was already expecting her.

At first glance Cora released this was the same boy who tried to form an alliance with Scarlet. His eyes lit up with recognition. "Your father is Corin Bowman from the Ironheart guild, right? I'm a huge fan."

"Um, thanks," Cora replied, not letting her guard down.

"Please make an alliance with me?" he begged, making a face that resembled a sad puppy.

Cora thought back to what Scarlet said earlier. "You are far too trusting Cora, someone is gonna take advantage of that." Cora couldn't help but believe despite their flaws that everyone had some good inside of them and even though people make mistakes they still believe they're doing the right thing.

"I accept your request for an alliance." Maybe she was making a mistake but he could end up being good ally and if he decided to turn on her she could easily take him out.

"Wow, really?" He said rubbing a hand on his neck. "I wasn't expecting someone as important as you to actually want to team up with me."

Cora didn't really think she was any more important than anyone else.

"I'm Zyler Ellis," he said as he extended a hand.

"Cora Bowman," she replied giving his hand a firm shake.

Zyler looked down at his watch. "We have to go now!" He exclaimed.

All of a sudden several people ambushed them. The pair ran as fast as they could. One competitor grabbed the hood of Zyler's sweatshirt, holding him back as she hit the target once. She attempted to hit it a second time, but Cora sliced the girl's hand opened with her sword, forcing her to let go.

Cora pointed to a house on the right signaling for them to regroup inside.

Zyler nodded and threw a smoke bomb behind them, blinding their opponents. The two of them make it safely inside the house. Little did they know they were not alone.

"They've entered the building begin phase two."

4

— · —

CHAPTER 4

S he wrote on the chalkboard vigorously. The sound of the chalk scraping against the board sent chills down her spine and she loved it, loved solving complex equations with ease. She was happy to feel useful.

"I just got word from down stairs that two people have entered the building," her sister said as she paced back and forth.

"Excellent," Val replied.

"Did you just say excellent? Maybe you shut yourself in your lab for too long because that's not even enough eliminations for even one of us to pass. Would you care to explain how that's excellent?" her sister said now standing only a few inches away.

Adriana, the older of the two girls was the leader of their guild, the White Diamonds, not because of her leadership skills but because of her social status. She acted like a leader, but in reality she was nothing without Val.

"More people will come soon," Val responded, not looking up from her chalkboard.

"For your sake I hope you're right," Adriana threatened.

"My calculations are always correct," Val responded.

"They've entered the building begin phase two," she said through her earpiece to the rest of the White Diamonds.

"I only take orders from Adriana," the girl on the other said.

She looked to Adriana who was just standing there looking smug. Val let out a frustrated sigh as she plopped herself down into the nearest chair and opened up her laptop to check the cameras she installed downstairs.

There were two competitors, just like she had predicted. There was a girl with blonde hair who had a sword attached to her belt. She was clearly aiming to be a warrior. There was also a boy. He was wearing some sort of googles on his head and he had several devices strapped to his belt. She couldn't tell what they were from her vantage point. She'd have to be ready for whatever he might try to use against them.

Adriana finally gave the orders for the White Diamonds to begin phase two. A girl, with a slingshot in her hand, crouched down on the on the roof of the house directly next to the one Cora and Zyler were in. She was ready to snipe the intruders.

Her first shot broke straight through the glass window almost hitting the blonde, but she dodged it effortlessly. It was clear to see she practiced. She was obviously going to need something stronger.

"Use the stun grenade," Val said over her earpiece. There was nothing but silence on the other side.

"Do as she says," Adriana said through her earpiece.

The girl threw the stun grenade through the broken window. After a brief electrical shock, Cora and Zyler were both frozen in place. The boy was just out of her view but she had a perfect shot at the girl. She fired her second shot hitting the dead center of the target giving the girl her first strike. They'd have to hurry, the effects of the stun grenade would run out soon.

Val checked her screen again but all she could see was grey smoke.

"What's going on down there?" Adriana asked.

"They must have used a smoke bomb of some sorts," Val replied. Val had to admit the smoke bombs seemed to be very good quality. She couldn't help but wonder what the boy used to make them.

"I'm sending the troops downstairs." Adriana said.

We have no idea what we're up against. If we send the rest of the girls down there it could leave us at a serious disadvantage," Val protested.

"You're not the one in charge here and if you have a problem with how I'm running things,you can try to pass this test by yourself!" Adriana snapped.

That's exactly what Val was about to do as she walked down the hidden staircase she had found earlier.A loud voice came over the speakers almost causing Val to shriek and give away her position.

"Our 50th competitor has just passed that means half of our spots are taken time is of the essence."

Val had a clear shot at the intruders and as far as she knew they had no idea she was here. Even if she managed to take both of them out she'd still have to take out one more person to pass but it was a start.

"Do you think Scarlet passed? the boy asked. Val had a perfect shot from her hiding place behind some old boxes. She plotted out her trajectory and took the shot hitting the bulls eye and giving him his second strike.

Now they both knew she was here. They pulled out their swords and began to charge towards her. Even though Val preferred science and mathematics she had become relatively skilled at sword fighting since her father insisted she learned self defense.

Val took a swing at the girl but she dodged. Val realized there was no attack that she knew that the girl couldn't counter in some way, so Val swung the sword at her again and again. The girl took a step back every time. Val noticed this pattern and used it to her advantage. Val had the girl backed into a corner.

She was prepared to make her next move until she felt something cold on her skin. The boy placed his sword on her neck.

"Listen lady, we've got swords and aren't afraid to use them we suggest you surrender now," he said.

Val tried to think of a way to escape but it was too risky. She had no choice.

"I surrender," she said dropping her sword on the ground and raising her hands. "But you should know there are 9 highly trained warriors in this building and 3 more standing guard outside. If you have any chance of beating them, I'd suggest using some sort of diversion to separate some of them from the group. You will have a better advantage if they're in smaller groups."

"Why are you telling us this?" the blonde girl asked.

"Because I recently quit that guild and nothing would bring me more pleasure than seeing them fail," Val responded.

"I don't trust her, Cora," the boy said.

"Do you have a plan to defeat them?" Cora asked.

"Yes." That was a lie. She had part of a plan but that would have to do for now.

"Let her go Zyler," Cora said, placing her hands on her hips.

"Are you serious?" he asked.

"She has a plan to beat them and we have no idea what what we're up against. She's our best chance at passing this test," she said.

Zyler removed the sword from her neck.

"So what is this plan of yours?" Zyler asked, not removing his hand from his sword.

"There are 12 members of the White Diamonds not including myself. There are 3 guards outside and 3 guards on each floor. My plan is the barricade the door so the outside guards can't get in. Then, we each take out one guard on each floor," Val explained. "We'll need to figure out a way to separate them from each other. I suggest we use some of Zyler's tech. If the rest of his inventions are as advanced as his smoke bombs, we should have no problem passing."

Zyler still refused to let go of his sword, but Val swore she almost saw him blush.

"I created these shock devices. if you place them on some-ones skin it will give them a small shock but it will knock them out cold," Zyler said reaching into his pocket and pulling out the devices and distributing them evenly. "These are similar to the stun grenades you used on us earlier," he said, gesturing towards Val.

"That means we'll have to fight them in close range," Val said, glancing at the stairs. Val wasn't sure she was ready to fight her own guild-mates, even if they never were fond of her. But she knew she had to. They could hear several sets footsteps upstairs. they all anxiously glanced at the staircase

"Who's is going to go first?" Cora asked.

"I'll go," Zyler said. "I already have two strikes. I was the least likely to pass anyway. You two are so talented and you deserve to make it into the Prestige Program."

"You don't have to sacrifice yourself for us. You deserve to be here as a much I do," Cora said placing a hand on his shoulder.

A wide smile spread across his face. "What are we waiting for?" he asked.

The trio ran up the stairs.

"We need you to create a distraction," Val said to Zyler.

"What should I say?" Zyler asked.

"Anything we only need a quick diversion," she replied.

"Quick catch that that cat it stole my wallet!" Zyler exclaimed pointing out the window.

They all stare at him with a look of pure confusion, which gave Val and Cora enough time to sneak up behind them. Val managed to get a shock device on one of the White Diamonds knocking her out. She tapped the target three times giving her her first elimination. She only needed two more.

"You filthy traitor!" One of the girls shouted as she pulled out her sword.

She swiped at Val. Val quickly dodged. She reached in her pocket to grab a shock device when the girl sliced open the pocket spilling them all over the floor.

She backed Val up into the wall.

"What are you gonna do know?" she asked.

Suddenly the girl collapsed on the floor. Cora had placed a device on her and had taken her out. Now they each had one elimination. The sound of footsteps echoed through the halls.

"Hello sister" Adriana said looking as arrogant as ever. "You have a lot of nerve betraying us for these imbeciles."

"I can take care of her, guys. You just worry about taking out the rest of the guards." Val said picking up a shock device.

"Are you sure?" Cora asked.

"I've got this," Val said.

Adriana let out a faint laugh. Cora and Zyler went up to the next floor. Adriana swiped the sword at her face so quickly she didn't have time to react. Val's face stung with pain. Adriana held Val by the collar of her shirt.

"How dare you betray me! I was the one who protected you all those years! I was the one got you into this guild! Everything you've accomplished is because of me,"

She said. "Don't you understand? You're nothing without me.

"You're wrong! All you ever did was hold me back. I never asked you to do those things for me and I don't need your protection!" Val declared.

Val jabbed her knee into Adriana's stomach causing her to double over in pain releasing Val from her clutches. Val placed the shock device on her neck knocking her unconscious.

"I'm sorry sister," she whispered as she struck her out.

The voice came over the loudspeakers again. "Only ten spots remaining."

5

CHAPTER 5

O ne of them lunged at Cora but she evaded her attack. Her opponent tried to slice her with her sword. Cora quickly ducked out of the way. She swept her leg across the floor tripping the other girl.

Cora had her opponent right where she wanted her, but then she saw the same shadowy figure that attacked her earlier. It's entire face was covered in something that resembled black bandages. All she could see were the cold lifeless yellow eyes staring back at her.

She didn't notice her opponent had gotten back up and grabbed her hands so she couldn't fight back. She hit Cora's target once giving her a second strike. She was about to give Cora her third strike when all of a sudden she was rendered unconscious.

"Val!" Cora never thought she'd be so excited to see someone she had only met that day. Cora hit her opponents target three times. Her own target lit up as a sign that she had passed thanks to Val.

"Are you okay?"   Val asked. "You totally zoned out for a moment there."

Cora was unsure of how to respond. How could she even explain what's been happening to her.

"I'm fine," she lied.

"Did you pass?" Cora asked Val.

Val turned around revealing her glowing target. "I guess the Prestige Program has two new members," Val said with a smile.

"Make that three," Zyler interjected. "My parents are gonna be so proud."

"Our 100th competitor has just passed we will not be accepting any more new members into the Prestige Program this year."

The trio walked back to the main hall. Once they got there they were sent to separate areas to receive their results.

Cora was sent to the same office she had been in earlier that day. Walking down these hallways again gave her chills. It felt like something might jump out and attack her at any moment. She walked as fast as she could until she reached the office door and let herself in.

"Congratulations," the woman said removing Cora's target.

"Thanks," Cora responded.

"Here are your results," the women said handing Cora a clipboard.

Cora was afraid to look. Her stomach turned with anxiety. What ever was written on this page will decide her destiny. She slowly opened her eyes.

Coraline Bowman: Warrior

was written in bold letters. Cora let out a happy squeal.

Cora went outside to wait for her father to pick her up. As soon as her father saw her, he ran up to her as fast as his damaged spine would allow him, nearly hurting himself in the process.

"I made it,"she said, hugging him.

"I knew you would," he respond.

On the drive home Cora's father told her all about his time in the Prestige Program, but Cora could hardly focus. She was so overwhelmed with everything that happened today.

"What's wrong sweetheart?" he asked.

"Nothing," Cora lied for the third time today.

"You can't fool me," he said. "Do you want to tell me what's going on or not?"

"Do you believe in ghosts?" she asked.

Her father let out a deep sigh. "I didn't until a few years ago. Back when I was a member of the guild we were hired by an old woman who lived next to the resting grounds. She claimed every night she would see a living shadow. She said it was searching for something and it wouldn't leave until it found what it was looking for. I thought she had lost her mind and so did the guild leader, so we sent some of our rookies to investigate. They were all found dead the next morning. After further investigation we found out that the shadow had been seen in several resting grounds all over Thessonia. Some records go back almost two hundred years."

"How is that possible?" Cora questioned.

"I don't know. Anyone who went looking for answers ended up dead the next morning."

"Did you find out what the shadow was looking for?"

"No."

Cora had more questions now than before. Could this be the same shadow that attacked her? Why did it want to know about the blood king? Why was it asking her of all people. Cora had thought she heard all of her father's stories about being a warrior but, for some reason he never told her this one.

They arrived back home very late into the night. Cora tiptoed up to her room being extra careful not to wake her mother and grandmother. Once she entered her room she accidentally knocked a pen of her desk and on to the floor. She got down on her knees to pick it up. Then saw a familiar glimmer under her bed.

The sword she had taken lay there untouched. She had nearly forgotten that she left it there. She quickly pulled it out and examined it.

I should probably put this back, she thought to herself.

She waited until her father was asleep to sneak back down to the study. Her heart was pounding so fast it felt like it was going to burst. As she flipped the switch to open the passage she thought about the boy trapped in crystal.

To her surprise when she reached the end of the passage the boy was no longer trapped at all.

6

CHAPTER 6

The dark figure stood facing the back wall muttering something she couldn't make out. He slowly turned to face her. Blood was pouring out from a cut on his face. When he saw her his eyes lit up for a brief moment.

He slowly walked towards her his metal leg clanking with every step. He was a considerable amount taller than her which made him that much more intimidating.

He squeezed her hands and pulled her closer.

"Why didn't you tell me?" he asked.

Cora had no idea how to respond. "Tell you what?"

"I would have listened!" he yelled.

Cora started to wonder if this was all a strange dream and when she woke up everything would be back to normal.

"I've always treated you well, Lily," he said refusing to make eye contact. Cora had no idea who Lily was. This guy was clearly delusional. He could hardly keep his eyes open there were several times he nearly fainted. He was delirious, a side effect of being trapped in the crystal for so long.

Cora had no idea what to do with him. Most places would be closed at this hour. She was going to play along until morning then she'd figure something out.

She tried to sneak him up to her room quietly, but his metal leg clanked loudly with with every step.

Luckily they didn't wake anyone.

Once they reached the room the boy collapsed on her bed.

"Good night Lily," he whispered.

"Good night," Cora responded sitting down on the edge of her bed. Today had officially become the weirdest day of her life.

Where was she going to sleep? Cora's mother would kill her if she found out she brought a strange boy in her room. Not even Dimitri was allowed in her room.

Tomorrow was her first day of warrior training and she hadn't slept at all the night before. She laid down on the opposite side of the bed. The bed was barley big enough to fit both of them.

She woke up the next morning the sun was shining so bright it lit up her entire room.

"It was all a bad dream," she told herself. She rolled over on to her back to see a sword pointed directly at her face.

"You think you can fool me!" he yelled. "Where's Lily?"

"I don't know," Cora replied.

"You're with Rivero just like everyone else aren't you!"

"I don't know who that is," Cora said. "I don't know anything about Lily or Rivero or anything you've said."

He scoffed. "Where are you from Rome, Greece?"

"I'm from Thessonia," she said quietly.

He placed his sword at his side and began to pace across the room.

"Where are we now?" he asked, still pacing.

"Silvershore, it's a small coastal town in northern Thessonia. You've probably never heard of it." Cora had a tendency to ramble when she was uncomfortable.

He stared out the window for a few moments then he spoke. "That's impossible I grew up in Silvershore and it looks nothing like this."

Cora had in lived Silvershore her entire life and it always looked like this.

"You must be a witch," he said with complete sincerity.

"What?"

"Rivero must have hired you cast some sort of spell on me so he could overthrow me!"

"Listen, two days ago I was wandering around my house and I happened to find a secret passage in my grandmother's study, that's when I saw you trapped in crystals like the ones at the resting grounds and I assumed that you were dead. So I kinda borrowed your sword but, when I went to return it, you were free."

He laughed at the absurdity of her statements. Then, he leaned in so they were eye to eye. It felt like his dark red eyes were staring straight into her soul.

"You mean to tell me you've never heard of Galen Rivero?"

"No!" she said, slightly frustrated this time.

He turned towards the door. "You may keep the sword, it is merely a backup, it's nothing on my real sword." He said dropping it on the floor.

He began to walk down the hallway.

"Where are you going?" she asked.

He gave no response.

"Hey!"

He walked down the stairs through the kitchen and out the back door.

"It was a pleasure meeting you," he said.

"I don't even know you're name!" Cora exclaimed.

He gave her a confused look and laughed. "I have important business to attend to and I ask that you don't follow me."

That sounded like a threat. He began to walk away.

"Wait," she called out to him.

"Cora it's time to go!" her mother called out to her.

"One second, Mom there's something I really need to take care of."

Cora glanced at the clock. She was late. She looked at the boy and then looked at the clock. She really had to go. She grabbed her sword and met her mom in the car. They two drove in silence for a few minutes then her mother spoke.

"You know I don't approve of your career choice but I hope you know that I just want to keep you safe. I don't know what I would do if something happened to you."

"It's okay, Mom I'll be extra careful."

The Prestige Program held their career training in an old castle that the royal family donated. Cora navigated her way though the halls. There were bright red tapestries with pictures of lions on them, hanging from the ceiling that perfectly complemented the ivory walls. There were also several statues of lions scattered throughout the halls. Whoever decorated this place had good taste. Cora thought to herself.

She followed her map to the back courtyard where the warrior training was to take place. The courtyard had a large fountain in the center and there were several bushes with white lilies lining the walls.

The teacher made all the students stand in a single file line, but out of the corner of her eye Cora could see Dimitri. Cora was so glad he made it. It wouldn't have been the same without him.

Every single muscle in her body ached, she had no idea the training would be this brutal. Mr. Tréville didn't hold back at all, but there was no way she was going to give up now.

Cora walked towards the break room dragging her feet behind every step of the way. She nearly tripped over her own feet on her way to the snack counter.

"Are you alright?" A somewhat familiar voice asked from behind her. It was Prince Lyon.

"I'm alright," she said as she placed a hand on her aching back.

"Here, take a seat," he said pulling out a chair.

Cora sat down. "What are you doing here?"

"I'm here to study the same as you."

"I mean what what are you doing in the break room don't you have a private room or something?"

"I do but, I haven't been to this castle in so long I thought I'd take a look around."

Prince Lyon took a few steps towards the counter.

"Where are my manners? May I get you a some tea?" he asked.

"I couldn't possibly ask you to do that for me," Cora started to ramble.

"Don't be ridiculous," he said with a wink. "You're wish is my command."

"I would like some tea," Cora said nervously.

A few moments later, Lyon returned with the tea.

Cora took a sip. It tasted like fresh herbs with a hint of cherry. It was so delicious Cora chugged the entire cup as fast as she could.

Prince Lyon let out a laugh. You're so funny, Cora," he said with huge smile.

For some reason her heart started pounding. Something about his laugh made her feel safe.

Cora felt a hand on her shoulder which snapped her back to reality.

"Hey Cora," Dimitri said.

"Hey!" Cora replied. "I've missed you."

"We saw each other yesterday," he said sitting down next to her.

"I know but a lot of stuff has been happening to me lately."

"What kind of stuff?"

"Weird stuff."

Scarlet just stood there with her arms crossed. Cora couldn't remember a time when Scarlet wasn't by her brother's side. Cora wondered if Scarlet ever did anything without her brother.

"You're in my diplomacy class right?" Prince Lyon asked Scarlet.

"Yes, my sorting results said I'll work in foreign negotiations," she said. Cora thought that was strange considering that she'd never seen Scarlet talk to anyone never mind negotiate.

Lyon checked his watch, which appeared to be made of solid gold. He let out an exasperated sigh. "I have to go I'll talk to you later, Cora, and if you ever need anything your wish is my command."

Prince Lyon gathered his things and walked out the door. Cora couldn't help but stare until he was out of sight.

"Where were we?" Cora asked Dimitri.

"Weird stuff."

"Right."

"Hey speaking of weird stuff did you see the news?" He questioned.

"No."

Dimitri pulled up a news article on his phone. The headline read:

MADMAN STEALS PRICELESS ARTIFACTS FROM ROYAL FAMILY.

The photo was blurry. It would be impossible for anyone else to make out but, to Cora it was clear as day. It was undoubtedly the boy she found trapped crystal.

Cora couldn't shake the feeling that this was all her fault. She had to find him and make things right. Nothing was going to stand in her way.

7

CHAPTER 7

He clearly had bad blood with someone named Galen Rivero. The more Cora thought about it the that name sounded familiar.

He seemed to be interested in royal artifacts but, Thessonia has so many historic locations it would be nearly impossible to predict which one he'd go for next.

Cora laid face down on her pillow. How was she gonna find this guy.

Cora needed to take a break. She got up to make her bed which she hasn't done in several weeks.

As she moved the blankets she found a small piece of white fabric. Upon further inspection she realized it was a handkerchief. It most definitely was not her's. There was a name embroidered on the bottom corner.

Raymundo Eduardo Esteban Ricardo Castillo V.

That must be him.

Cora immediately entered the name into the search bar. The Blood King. There were several paintings of The Blood King. There was no doubt about it, It was him.

In the paintings you could see battlefields covered in dead bodies. Blood stained the snow red. Some of them were so gruesome they made her sick. And there he was at the center of it all. He seemed to be enjoying himself slaughtering all those people.

The young man in this picture seemed different from the one she had met, but what did she know.

The more she thought about it, the more it made sense. His long hair, his sword, it would explain why he was confused as to how Cora didn't recognize him.

How was he still alive. Wasn't he killed 2,000 years ago? Even if he somehow survived, how come he didn't age at all?

Cora read several articles about the Blood King.

Raymundo Eduardo Esteban Ricardo Castillo the fifth, more commonly known as the Blood King, was born in the year 12 A.D. He was the only heir to the throne. He was crowned king at age ten after his father died in battle and his mother died due to unknown circumstances. He took more lives than any other king in Thessonian history. He conquered several of the surrounding nations. He married duchess Lilliana Rowe but, their marriage was cut short because the Blood King was killed at age eighteen by Galen Rivero. Three years later Duchess Lilliana married Rivero. There is currently a Blood King exhibit at the Thessonian Museum of History which features the real blade used by the Blood King.

That must be where he's going.

Since Cora didn't own a car she had to walk to the museum. The warm summer breeze washed over her. She had no idea what she would say to him when she found him but, it was too late to go back now.

Cora arrived at the museum late into the night. It was closed. She would have to be creative. She scaled over the museum's front gates landing on her feet on the other side.

Cora walked to the front door and tugged the handle. It was locked.

Cora walked around the back of the museum looking for a way in, when she realized one of the windows had been shattered. Cora climbed through the broken window being careful not to cut herself.

It was so dark she could hardly see anything. She felt her way through the darkness nearly stumbling several times.

"Hey you!" She turned around to see a security guard running towards her. She'd been caught. Cora bolted down the hall as fast as she could and he followed after her.

"Come back here!" he yelled.

Cora ran into a room on the right and slammed the door behind her. She grabbed a chair and used it to barricade the door. She let out a sigh of relief as she sat down in the chair. That's when she saw a pair of red eyes staring at her from the darkest corner of the room.

"I told you not to follow me," he said, taking a step towards a glass case with a sword twice the size of the one from the passage. "You are a fool for coming here."

He smashed through the glass with his fist. Cora's throat went completely dry she couldn't make a sound. All she could do was stand in silence, completely frozen.

He grabbed the sword off the shelf and gripped it tightly in his hand.

"You look like you have something you want to say to me." He was now standing only a few inches away from her.

"You're the Blood King," she whispered, barely audible.

"I hate that name!" he yelled.

He tried to stab her in the abdomen but, out of pure instinct she pulled out her sword and blocked the incoming attack.

"I've met very few with reflexes as fast as yours," he said with a look of amusement in his eyes. He refused to yield he slashed her shoulder.

The pain caused her to flinch. She quickly dodged his next attack. Her sweatshirt was now soaked in blood. Cora tried to think of what she could say to calm his rage.

"Lily wouldn't have wanted you to do this."

He paused. For a brief moment there was a look of sorrow in his eyes. Then he snapped. "Lily was the one who tried to kill me! She was the one who trapped me in those crystals for 2,000 years! Don't pretend like you know her!"

Cora threw a vase at him shattering it into a thousand pieces. He let out a wince in pain. Cora launched an attack aiming for his face. He grabbed her wrist and twisted it. The pain overwhelmed her and she was forced to drop her sword.

"Any last words?"

8

— · —

CHAPTER 8

Cora was completely immobilized. There was nothing she could do. It couldn't end like this!

"No?"

The harder Cora tried to break free the tighter his grip became. The pain was becoming unbearable.

Cora kicked him in the shin causing him to let go.

She picked her sword up off the ground. He attempted to punch her. Cora ducked out of the way.

He punched a hole in the wall and knocked a painting down in the process. Cora tried to use the painting as a shield but he sliced it in half.

Cora attacked again and again but, he deflected every attack. He was much too skilled with the sword. Cora could never beat him on her own. That's when her eyes drifted to a statue in the center of the room. She had an idea.

With every on of his attacks Cora took a step towards the statue. When she was close enough she pushed the statue as hard as she possibly could using all the strength left in her until she knocked it over on top of him crushing his metal leg.

He tried desperately to get up but he couldn't. He tried to be strong but it was clear he was in pain. He was forced to remove his metal leg just for some relief.

Cora kicked his sword far away from his reach then she also collapsed on the floor from exhaustion. The pair sat in silence. There was something peaceful about it even though it was only a few minutes it felt much longer to them.

Then the boy spoke. "Finish your mission."

Cora just stared at him in silence unsure of how to respond.

"This was your mission wasn't it? Didn't your guild send you on a mission to kill me?"

"I don't kill people," was the only response she could think of.

He laughed. "Don't worry I've done terrible things you'll be able to sleep at night knowing the world has one less murderer."

Cora said nothing.

"End me!" he yelled with something that resembled tears in his eyes. "I don't deserve to live."

Cora's knees wobbled as she stood up. she walked over to him and stretched out her hand. "Like I said I don't kill people and no one sent me here. I just want to talk to you."

Then there was a sound coming from the door. The guard was finally managing to break through the barricade. He quickly reattached his metal leg and she helped him stand. Cora opened the window and they climbed out together and left the sword behind.

The duo hid in the bushes outside until the security guards left. They walked back to Cora's house in complete silence. Cora escorted him into the guest house far behind her house. Her family never had guests so no one ever went in the guest house.

Once they entered the house he dropped down on one knee and kissed her hand. "I must apologize for the trouble I've caused you, I thought you were hired to kill me so I defended myself. I hope one day you will forgive me."

"Don't worry about it," Cora responded slightly embarrassed by the whole ordeal.

"How may I address you?" He asked.

"My name is Coraline Bowman."

"That's a beautiful name."

He rose to his feet and looked around the room for the first time. The room was fairly small. There was nothing in it besides a bed and a small grey sofa and there was a small bathroom attached to the house. It was enough for someone to live in but, he was probably expecting something much fancier.

To Cora's surprise he smiled.

There was a loud thud outside that made Cora yelp and jump backwards. A dead tree branch had fallen.

He laughed at her. "I would thought a warrior capable of taking me down wouldn't be such a coward."

Cora's blood boiled. She considered punching him in the face but decided against it. "If you knew what's been happening to me lately you'd know I have a right to be afraid!"

"Then tell me."

She didn't even know how to begin to explain. "A shadow attacked me a couple of days ago he said he was looking for you, I barely escaped and feel like it's been following me ever since."

"It was looking for me?"

"It wanted to know everything I knew about the Blood King."

He just nodded slowly. He took a seat on the bed. "Don't worry, I'm scarier than anything out there," he said with a grin that resembled the Cheshire Cat.

Cora wondered if that was true, she had no idea what she was getting herself into.

"What should I call you?" she asked.

"I don't know, everyone calls me your your majesty or your highness."

Cora put her hands into her pockets. She felt a small piece of fabric, the handkerchief. She had completely forgotten about it. There it read

Raymundo Eduardo Esteban Ricardo Castillo V.

She handed it to him. "Is that your name?"

"Yes, but I always thought it was a bit too extravagant for me."

"What about Ray?"

"What?"

"Can I call you Ray?"

He mouthed out the name silently a few times. "You may call me Ray if you would like to."

Cora's phone rang.

"Where are you?" Her mother said sounding horrified.

"I'm hanging out with a friend." That wasn't a complete lie. "Don't worry I'll be home soon."

"Listen, your grandmother was stabbed." Cora's head started spinning. This was too much for her to handle.

"What happened?" Cora eventually managed to ask.

"No one knows, we found her in her study with a knife in her chest. In the security footage there was nothing but a shadow."

9

— · —

CHAPTER 9

"We've managed to stabilize her but, we don't know how long it will last," one of the doctors said.

"Can I see her?" Cora asked.

"Go ahead."

She squeezed her grandmother's hand tightly. Her eyes filled up with tears.

"The Blood King has returned," her grandmother whispered. "The end is near."

"What are you talking about?"

"The King of Shadows will not rest until he has found what he is looking for."

Cora had so many questions. How did her grandmother know about the Blood King? How did she know he was no longer trapped? Who is The King of Shadows? Is he the one that's been attacking them?

"What is he looking for?" Cora asked.

Her grandmother let out a loud laugh. "He'll never find what he's looking for."

"I need you to tell me what's going on!" Cora said desperately searching for answers.

"I thought I could protect you by locking him away but I see now that was never the answer."

"What are you saying?"

"You're a warrior, it's in your blood. I know you'll be able to stop the Armageddon. I'm counting on you." Her grandmother squeezed Cora's hand tightly until the steady beat on the heart rate monitor slowed to a stop.

Cora couldn't hold back her sobs. This couldn't be happening. She tried to pull herself together but, there was nothing she could possibly do to stop the tears for cascading down.

She was going to kill whoever did this!

Cora spent the rest of the day in her room trying to plot her revenge but, she always ended up in tears. Her father knocked on her door.

"Someone's here to see you but I can tell them to leave if you're not up to it," he said.

It was probably Dimitri.

She wiped her tears and stood up. "It's okay I need someone to talk to."

When she walked down the stairs she was shocked to see Prince Lyon accompanied by two burley men who appeared to be his bodyguards.

Cora was so nervous she couldn't speak. The prince of Thessonia was in her house.

"On behalf of the royal family I would like to offer my condolences to the family of Corona Bowman. She was a noble warrior who served the royal family for many years."

"Thank you," was all Cora managed to say.

"I brought you some tea," Prince Lyon said raising a cup in the air.

Cora quickly walked down the last few steps bridging the gap between them. She took the cup from his hands and took a huge gulp. She had been craving tea all day.

"This must very hard for you I want you to know that you can tell me anything," he said as he placed his hand on hers.

Cora could feel herself blushing. Cora wasn't usually the type to get flustered. Why was she blushing? The phone of one of his guards rang. He picked it up, nodded, then whispered something in Lyon's ear.

He frowned. "I have business to attend to. There's trouble on Mt. Nevado. I hope you understand. Don't worry I'll see you again soon."

Cora went to warrior training the next day despite her mother's disapproval. Her grandmother would have wanted her to go. Ray had begged to go with her.

"No! What if someone recognizes you?" is what she said. The last thing Cora needed was one more thing to worry about.

Cora was exhausted she hadn't had a good night's sleep since before this whole ordeal started and it showed during her training today. She was falling behind. She wasn't going to get offers to join any guilds at this rate.

Mr. Tréville said something about splitting up into pairs but Cora wasn't really paying attention. Dimitri walked over to her with a smile, his face fell when he came closer. "You look awful," he said.

"My grandmother just died how am I supposed to look?" Cora snapped.

"I'm sorry I didn't know."

"It's alright."

The duo trained in silence until class ended.

Then Dimitri finally broke the silence. "I received a request to join the Ruby Python guild yesterday."

"Aren't they the second best guild in western Thessonia?" Cora asked as her blue eyes widened with excitement.

"Yep. Did you get any requests yet?"

"No," Cora's heart sank she always thought she and Dimitri were on the same level but apparently he was ahead of her. This meant she had to train harder. A guild would notice her eventually.

Cora began her walk to through the courtyard towards the break room. She hadn't eaten anything today and she felt fatigued because of it. Her vision became blurred. She could feel her consciousness fading. She started to black out until she felt someone catch her.

She didn't recognize who caught her until he spoke. "Are you alright, Coraline?"

"Ray?"

He looked completely unrecognizable. He was wearing a Metallica tank top and ripped jeans. He had cut his hair. It now fell above his eyes. One side was longer than the other. It was easy to tell he did himself. He still had the same red eyes and mischievous grin.

She was so distracted she didn't notice that he was still holding her.

"I'm okay," she said regaining her footing. "What are you doing here?"

"Please don't be mad at me. I know you told me not to come here but, I must ask you a favor." He sounded so awkward. Cora found it so hard to believe that this was the Blood King. The person that struck fear in the hearts of everyone who heard his name. Cora wanted to laugh but she didn't.

"I'm not mad," she said sitting down on the grass. "What do you need?"

He sat down next to her even though his metal made it difficult. That's when Cora noticed he was holding two bags of food from the break room.

"I need you to ask your magic mirror about something."

"My what?"

"Your magic mirror. The one that you stare at all day!" He exclaimed gesturing to her pocket.

"My phone?"

"Is that what you call it?"

Cora let out a sigh. "What would you like to know?"

"I want to know if Lily was happy with Rivero."

The blonde stared down at her phone. "I don't think it can tell me that," She said.

He frowned.

"Did you love her?" Cora asked and then immediately regretted it.

To her surprise he said. "No. I didn't. It was an arranged marriage. I was just going along with my mother's wishes. Lily was never happy with me. On the day we met she told me that I was repulsive. I thought I could make things work between us but I was wrong. I just hope he was good enough for her."

All Cora could say was. "I'm sorry."

"Don't be."

He opened up one of the bags. There was a turkey sandwich an apple and a bag of Doritos inside. He examined the bag of Doritos. "How is one supposed to eat this?" He asked.

Cora took the bag from his hands opened it pulled one out and ate it. Ray grabbed one and ate it. He chewed it for a long time. Then he grabbed the bag out of her hands. "I like these very much." He handed her the other bag.

"Hey what do you know about the King of Shadows," Cora asked casually.

Ray laughed. "The King of Shadows is a tale parents tell to children to make them behave. He brings love and wealth for the good and punishes the evil."

"Like santa clause."

Ray shrugged. "No one has ever seen him. I don't believe he's real"

This didn't make Cora feel any better. Someone or something killed her grandmother and she was going to find them. Ray seemed to be disinterested so she changed the subject.

"You look really nice," Cora said.

"You really think so?" He asked nervously running a hand through his hair.

"Totally."

The pair enjoyed their lunch together.

As they were cleaning up Zyler came running up to them holding a flyer.

"Cora!" He called out gasping for air.

"What's happening?" Cora asked. She hadn't seen Zyler or Val since the Sorting. She wondered why Zyler would come looking for her.

"I'll tell you what happening I'm putting the team back together!" He held up the flyer. "Mount Nevado is being attacked by killer wolves!"

Cora took the flyer and read it.

Tibicenas attack mountain village.

A pack of magical wolves known as Tibicenas have awakened from their hibernation early. No one knows what awoke these creatures but several villagers reported strange activity around their den. The usually timid creatures have begun to attack the people of the village and steal from their food supply.

There is a reward of 4,000 Euros to whomever manages to stop them.

"Val said maybe. Please come with me for old times sake."

None of them were qualified for this mission. Cora was surprised Val was considering it.

Cora took a close look at the photograph on the flyer. It was a pack of giant wolves with glowing red eyes and blood stained fur. In the distance she saw a familiar pair of yellow eyes who seemed to be enjoying the bloodshed.

It made her angry.

"I'm in."

10

CHAPTER 10

It would be impossible for someone to tell that it was mid June on Mt. Nevado. The group trudged through the knee deep fresh snow. There were no other signs of life anywhere. A harsh wind blew through the frosty atmosphere, which made Cora shiver.

Several snowflakes had landed in her hair, making it damp, which only made her colder. "What's our strategy?" Cora asked loud enough to be heard over the howling wind.

"I brought bones. Tibicenas are like big dogs, so they should like bones right?" Zyler asked.

"In my experience they eat the flesh and leave the bones behind," Ray corrected.

Cora didn't know how Ray had convinced her to let him come with them, but if she was honest with herself, she was glad he came.

"Hey Cora, who is your friend and why does he know so much about Tibicenas?" Val asked.

"My name is Ray Castillo and I had one as a pet once. It had a tendency to bite people that owed me money," Ray responded.

"I have so many questions about this guy," Zyler said anxiously.

"I'm surprised you came, Val," Cora said trying to change the subject.

"Well, things aren't great at home right now. Adriana hasn't acknowledged me since the Sorting,"

"I'm sorry," Cora said, blaming herself for some reason.

"Don't be, I had been planning on standing up to her for a long time," Val reassured her.

Zyler winced in pain as a vine with huge thorns grabbed onto his ankle causing blood to come rushing out. Cora quickly severed the vine forcing it to release its grasp.

"What was that?" Zyler asked.

"That was a Death Vine. It's carnivorous plant that only grows on Mt. Nevado. It's insides can be used to make potions, medicines and other things," Val explained.

Cora was distracted by a tracks left in the snow. There were four sets of paw prints bigger than her hands. The Tibicenas were larger that she had previously thought. There were also two sets of human footprints. One of them looked like they had been there for a long time and the other looked more recent like they had been made only a few minutes ago.

The group continued long the frozen path.

Snow had gotten into Cora's boots making them very uncomfortable. She hated the cold. She pulled her coat closer to her chest.

Ray removed his cape and draped it around her shoulders. "Don't worry we're almost there," he whispered into her ear.

Cora saw a flash of red in one of the trees but it quickly disappeared. Cora gripped her sword tightly. No one was going to catch her off guard again.

Cora looked straight ahead. They were approaching the village. The only thing that was separating them was a bridge made completely out of ice. It stretched across and icy canyon. One wrong move and you would fall to your death.

The party was startled by the sound of growls from behind them. There was an entire pack of Tibicenas ready to attack.

"Hey! Are you hungry?" Zyler called out offering them a bone. They refused to take their eyes off Ray.

One of the Tibicenas pounced at Ray. Cora kicked it sending it flying into a snow bank. She was going to try her hardest not to kill them, the shadow clearly had some sort of control over them, but she couldn't let any harm come to her friends.

The pack closed in on them. The group was forced to step onto ice bridge. Cora couldn't help but look down into the icy ravine she had no idea how they were going to make it out of this alive.

The wolves weren't going to give up so easily. They charged towards Ray. One of them managed to rip of Val's bag and dropped it off the edge.

The bridge wasn't strong enough to handle this much weight and it began to crack.

"Zyler, do have any of the shock devices you had at the Sorting?" Val asked.

Zyler rummaged through his pockets. "I only have three."

There were eight wolves on the bridge they'd have to improvise.

Cora quickly grabbed a device from Zyler's pocket and threw it at the largest one knocking it unconscious.

Cora jumped in front of Ray. "Get out of here I'll hold them off!"

"I can't let you die for me," he said, his voice sounding broken.

"I can handle them. Everyone, get to the village!" Cora wasn't sure if she could handle them but she had to try.

Zyler threw the other two devices in her direction and she caught them effortlessly in her left hand. The rest of the group ran across the bridge leaving Cora alone against the pack. The pack charged towards her. Cora stood her ground. She wasn't going down without a fight.

The first one jumped in an attempt to bite Cora's face. She placed a device on its chest. There was only one device left and five Tibicenas. One clawed at her chest while another bit her leg. She tried her hardest to fight back but the pack piled on top of her.

In the distance she could see a figure in a bright red hood walking towards her. It was much shorter than the shadow. The figure whistled loudly gaining the attention of the Tibicenas. They turned to the figure and began to attack.

Once they got close, the cloaked stranger started saying something Cora couldn't understand which seemed to slightly calm them down then injected something into their necks.

After the stranger injected all of the Tibicenas it carefully removed the shock devices and bandaged any injuries they had received.

Cora's wounds throbbed with pain and it only got worse and she stood up. The Tibicenas followed closely after the stranger. They no longer seemed vicious.

The figure spoke. "They will no longer hurt you, I suggest that you go home Cora you're way out of your league. You have no idea what you're up against."

Cora recognized that voice. She couldn't control her impulses. She had to know if her suspicions were correct. She pulled off the strangers hood.

"Scarlet?"

11

CHAPTER 11

The doctor was a small elderly lady. "I don't know what you were thinking trying to take on a whole pack of Tibicenas alone. I can't tell if you're brave or stupid," she said as she applied bandages to the bite on her shoulder.

Scarlet let out a faint chuckle under her breath. She knelt on the floor next to a dog bed with a small St. Bernard puppy inside. "Come here, boy," she said.

"Don't bother," the doctor said. "That damn dog doesn't listen to a word anyone says."

To her surprise the dog got up and ran to Scarlet.

"Now sit. Lie down. Roll over."

The dog obeyed all of her commands.

"Good boy!" Scarlet exclaimed. She reached into her pocket and pulled out a treat and fed it to the dog.

The doctor stood there with her jaw dropped. "I haven't taught him any tricks yet!"

"Maybe he knows more than you think," Scarlet replied.

"You've got some sort of gift," the doctor said as she finished taking care of Cora.

Cora and Scarlet walked to the inn the where Scarlet was staying. Scarlet refused to say anything or make eye contact.

The inside resembled a log cabin. The walls and floor were made out of hard wood. There was a dark red rug and three armchairs that surrounded a fireplace. The inn smelt like a mix of spruce wood and cinnamon. The whole place felt warm and inviting.

Val, Zyler and Ray had stayed up waiting for her at the inn.

"Thank God you're alive!" Val exclaimed.

They escorted her to the nearest chair and she sat down.

"How did you manage to take on an entire pack of Tibicenas and live to tell the tale?" Zyler asked.

"I'm not entirely sure," Cora responded gesturing to Scarlet. "What did you do?"

"I stopped you from doing something stupid," Scarlet responded. "You don't understand what's going on here."

"Then explain it to me!" Cora said raising her voice.

Scarlet reached into her pocket and pulled out a vile. It was almost empty. There was only one drop of red liquid in the bottom.

"This was a Bloodshed Potion. Just one drop can drive anyone mad. Someone poured this into the Tibicenas water supply. I don't know who did this but I do know that this was sabotage."

Cora knew exactly who did this but why did he do it? All she knew was he was looking for something. What could be worth all the trouble he's going through?

"How do you know all this?" Val asked.

"I have a rare connection with animals. I can feel what they feel and communicate with them to some extent but it doesn't work on fish or insects." Scarlet said. "I knew something was wrong when the Tibicenas started attacking people so I came here to investigate."

Cora had heard of people with similar abilities Scarlet's mother being one of them. It was now that Cora realized how little she actually knew about Scarlet.

"You're like a Disney princess! That's so cool!" Zyler exclaimed.

Scarlet rolled her eyes. "I knew someone was going to show up and try to collect the reward without asking any questions and kill the Tibicenas thinking that they just randomly went crazy. When I saw you coming up the mountain I followed you to make sure that didn't happen," Scarlet continued. "I had made the antidote a few days prior but they wouldn't let me get close enough to inject it until I saved Cora on the bridge."

"Why should I trust you?" Cora asked.

"If I wanted you dead I would have let the Tibicenas eat you."

"Does Dimitri know you're here?" Cora asked.

"Dimitri doesn't know a lot of things,"

"Bloodshed is one of the most complicated potions to create and it's illegal in every country in Europe. If it was sabotage, whoever's behind this must be an expert at potion making," Val said checking her notes.

"Does it matter if it was sabotage or not? It's over. Scarlet gave them the antidote," Zyler said.

"It's not over. That wasn't even half of the pack. The rest of them are in the den just waiting to attack." Scarlet said.

"Then we need to attack first," Cora interjected.

Zyler let out a yawn. "Can we do that tomorrow?"

It was very late.

Val started writing vigorously in her notebook. "I should have a plan by the morning,"

"Goodnight," Scarlet said exiting the lobby and heading for her room.

"If you guys don't need me I'm gonna go too," Zyler said.

"Go ahead," Val said. "I'm gonna head to my room and work on our strategy."

Cora began to leave when Ray gently grabbed her hand.

"Can we talk for a moment?" he asked.

"Sure,"

Ray hadn't said a word since the bridge. The light from the fire illuminated his tan skin. As Cora came closer she could see tear stains on his face.

"You shouldn't have risked your life for me," he said. "I'm not worth it."

"What are you talking about? Of course you are!"

"I'm a monster, Coraline. Everyone knows that! I don't know why but, for some reason you believed in me. You looked at me and saw something more than that. You're the first person I've ever considered to be my friend and if I lost you..." He choked up and couldn't manage to finish that sentence.

Cora almost involuntarily wrapped her arms around his waist and held him tight. She rested her head on his chest. She could hear the steady rhythm of his heartbeat.

He returned her embrace then pulled her even closer. They stood there in silence for several minutes. Cora felt so safe and warm in his arms and she never wanted to let go.

Ray ran his fingers through her hair. "I don't deserve you," he whispered.

"You say that you're a monster but since that night at the museum you've been nothing but kind to me. The Ray I know is a gentleman not a tyrant," Cora said.

Ray let go of her and sat down in the closest chair and Cora sat down next to him.

"Have you ever heard of the Revolution of Golden Crest?" he asked.

She shook her head.

"My subjects weren't pleased with how I was ruling Thessionia. I had heard that some people in a city called Golden Crest were planning to try to dethrone me. I underestimated them and it cost me my leg. I was only ten at the time. I let my rage cloud my judgment." Ray stared at the floor in shame.

"What did you do?" Cora asked placing a hand on his shoulder.

"I burned the city to the ground. There were no survivors."

Cora didn't know how to process this information. She knew that the Blood King did horrible things but for some reason she had a hard time believing that Ray really killed that many people.

"My mother stabbed herself through the heart when she saw what I had become." He said with tears dripping down his face. "I understand if you don't want anything to do with me,"

"I'm mad at you for killing those people, but it's clear that you're not the same person you were then," Cora said.

"You truly are one in a million, Coraline."

Cora's eyes were getting heavy. It was impossible to hide her exhaustion.

"You should get some rest," Ray said. Then kissed her hand.

Cora was heading to her room when she saw a news report on the TV at the hotel bar.

Prince Lyon Attacked on Route to Mt. Nevado.

No one knew how how badly injured he was. Cora couldn't stop thinking about him on the walk to her room.

She unlocked her door and entered the room.

To her surprise a familiar shadow stood in the middle of the room. His yellow eyes ripped through her soul.

"Cora Bowman, I think it's time that we have a little chat."

12

— • —

CHAPTER 12

Cora pulled out her sword ready to defend herself.

He vanished into the darkness. She frantically looked around the room trying to figure were he disappeared to. He tried to grab her from behind. She was never going to let him touch her ever again.

She spun around and swung her sword at him. He caught the blade between his thumb and index finger.

"You're too slow," he said.

Cora tightened her grip on the sword's handle and tried to rip it out of his grasp.

"I'd listen to what I have to say if I were you," he said, removing his sword from the sheath. "I won't hesitate to slaughter you where you stand."

Cora stopped struggling. He ran the tip of his sword back and forth across her neck. "The old hag wouldn't give me what I want. Let's hope you'll cooperate."

Cora's blood boiled. This was the man that murdered her grandmother. He stood right in front front of her and she couldn't lay a finger on him. He was too fast.

"What do you want?" she asked, trying to mask the anger in her voice.

He leaned so close. He was only a couple of centimeters away from her face. He smelled like burning sulfur. There was a look of pure insanity in his glowing, yellow eyes. "I want the Blood King's head on a silver plate."

Cora couldn't breathe. He wanted to kill Ray!

"We both know he's a mad man," he said, pacing back and forth.

Cora thought about Golden Crest. He burned the entire city to the ground out of pure anger.

"I know that you know where he is and I won't hesitate to kill every single one of you're friends until I have him. Prince Charming will be the first to go."

Prince Lyon!

"I let him live this time but I won't be so generous next time."

Cora couldn't remember the last time she was completely frozen, incapable of doing anything at all. She just stood there in shock.

"Then I'll move on to the rest of them Dimitri and Zyler and Val and Scarlet. How is it going to feel having their lives on your conscience." He pointed his sword at her face. "Then, If you still don't cooperate, I'll kill you too. If you won't meet my demands, maybe your father will."

Cora wanted to kill him. She wanted to make him to suffer but she couldn't do anything.

"You have until my return to make your decision." And just like that he vanished into the darkness of night.

Cora collapsed on the cold wooden floors. She couldn't stop trembling.

The answer should be simple. The Blood King was ruthless. He burned cities to the ground and killed everyone in them. She couldn't stop thinking about Ray's mischievous smile and warm embrace and his handsome face and the way his words always managed to comfort her. Why was this so hard?

Cora tiptoed down the halls. It was long past midnight. Once she reached the room she was looking for she gently knocked on the door. She shouldn't be doing this, he was probably asleep.

"Come in," the voice on the other side said.

Cora slowly opened the door. His face lit up like Christmas the moment he saw her. "Coraline, to what do I owe the pleasure of seeing you tonight?"

Ray was sitting on top of his bed. His artificial leg was leaned up against nightstand beside the bed. He held an open book in his hands, Romeo and Juliet.

Cora tried to speak but, she couldn't think of the right words to say, so she just stood there.He closed his book and patted the spot next to him on the bed. "Sit with me."

She sat down beside him. He wrapped a blanket around her. "Tell me everything,"

Cora didn't know where to start. "The shadow was in my room,"

"Are you sure it wasn't a dream?"

"Yes!"

He rubbed her shoulders. Cora had been in pain since the Tibicena attack. The feeling of Ray's soft fingers massaging her felt amazing. "What did he say?"

"He said if I didn't turn you over to him he'd kill me and all of my friends!"

"I swear to you on my life no harm will come to you or your friends."

"That's what I'm afraid of," she murmured.

He let out a long deep breath. " Some of the greatest assassins in Thessionia have tried to kill me. I've gone up against hundreds of foes that all wanted me dead, but none of them succeeded. This shadow is no different. Plus, I have the bravest warrior in all of Thessionia on my side."

Cora was feeling a little bit better. Ray's room was so much warmer than her own. He stared at her with a longing look in his eyes. Cora brushed his hair out of his eyes. Short hair suited him. He seemed to be adjusting well considering he was trapped for so long. She couldn't let him die. "I won't let him hurt you,"

"I know you won't."

Cora was afraid. Afraid of the shadow. Afraid of what he'll do. Afraid of losing Ray. Maybe she was being selfish by not giving up Ray but, she was sure she would find a way to stop the shadow and save everyone.

"You're more than welcome to stay here if you'd like," he said.

The thought of going back to her room made her shiver. She could stay just a little bit longer.

Cora woke up the next morning with Ray's cape wrapped around her. Cora got out of her bed. Ray had stayed with her until she fell asleep. Just thinking about him made her feel warm inside.

Did she have feelings for Ray? This was all happening so fast and at such a bad time. And what about Prince Lyon.

Prince Lyon! He was attacked last night! She had completely forgotten.

She ran to the doctor's hut. She had slept in her clothes and didn't bother to change. She had to see Prince Lyon. They probably wouldn't let her talk to him but she didn't care at the moment.

When Cora arrived at the doctors hut, it was empty. The doctor entered through the back door.

"Where's Prince Lyon?"

"His royal highness left a while ago."

"How is he doing?"

"He's in rough shape but he'll heal eventually."

Cora's heart sank. "Do you know where he went?"

"I don't believe I'm allowed to hand out that information."

"Please! I need to see him!" Cora begged.

The old woman turned away. She said nothing for a few moments then she spoke. "He said something about going to the library."

"Thank you!"

The doctor murmured something about fangirls as Cora left.

She ran to the village library as fast as her feet would carry her. Cora slowly opened the door afraid of what she would see.

The library was a very old building. The floor creaked as Cora walked. Several large bookcases lined the walls. In the center of the room there stood a long wooden table surrounded by chairs.

Prince Lyon sat in the farthest chair from the door. He was surrounded by a several stacks of books. Only one of his guards was with him. One eye was completely covered in bandages. His face was bruised and swollen. He forced his best smile when he saw her. "Don't tell me you climbed Mt. Nevado just to see me," he teased.

"Nope, I'm here on warrior business."

His face went serious. "Don't you think you're in over your head?"

Cora's heart shattered. He was right. She was way out of her league. She was no match for the Tibicenas. But Ray was always so confident in her abilities.

"I just don't want you to get hurt," he said. He tried his hardest to stand but the pain overwhelmed him. Cora offered him her hand, but the guard slapped it away. "Forgive him, we've all been a bit paranoid since Richard, my other guard was killed by the Tibicenas."

"I'm so sorry."

"He was a good man. He had a family. I swear I'm going to bring whoever did this to justice!"

Cora wasn't convinced. Lyon didn't know who he was up against. She turned towards the bookshelf.

It felt like it was calling out to her. A book titled Armageddon. She picked it up off the shelf and admired the cover. It was a shade of royal blue with a silver sword in the middle. The cover read.

Armageddon by Corona Bowman.

Cora had no idea her grandmother had written a book. She opened it to the first page.

It said.

Dear Cora, if you're reading this than the Armageddon has already begun and my time has ended. The King of Shadows has come to for the Blood King. For the last 2,000 years it has been our family's secret duty to protect the Blood King. Once the kings clash, all of Thessionia will be overrun with darkness. I thought I was protecting you by keeping the Blood King trapped but I now realize that I was afraid of him. You were not. In that way you are a greater warrior than I ever was. You saw the good in him no one else could. The King of Shadows' mind has been corrupted by darkness. He believes he'll finally be satisfied once he has his revenge but he is wrong. I have faith you will stop him. I love you Cora.

13

— · —

CHAPTER 13

She sat in the nearest chair.

Prince Lyon placed a hand on her shoulder. "You seem preoccupied. Should we talk another time."

Cora shut the book. "No, I just got distracted for a moment."

"Unfortunately I'm all out of tea."

Cora felt a small twinge of disappointment but she understood. "Don't worry about it, you've had a rough couple of days."

"Maybe this will make up for it," he placed a small opened box in front of her. Inside was a silver bracelet covered in diamonds in the center there was flower that appeared to be made completely out of sapphires.

"It's beautiful! I can't accept this. I mean you're the prince. I shouldn't even be allowed to talk to someone like you." She was rambling again.

"I am no more important than anyone else especially you."

Technically that was false but, Cora understood what he was trying to say. She slipped it on. "Thank you."

You're most welcome."

Cora gazed into his eyes expecting to feel bubbly inside like she always did around him. Nothing. She felt nothing. She used to dream about falling in love with a handsome prince and here she was and she felt nothing.

She glanced at the clock on the back wall. She had to leave soon. "I need to go," she whispered refusing to meetups gaze.

"Go ahead then."

She checked out the book then left for the den. She and her friends were going to stop the Tibicenas once and for all.

She trudged through knee deep snow until she was deep into the woods. She had no clue how people could live in this climate.

The den was a huge cave made entirely out of ice. It was so dark Cora couldn't tell exactly how large it was. The longest icicles she had ever seen clung to the ceiling. They were sharp enough to impale someone upon contact. She heard the faint sound of howling. She was unsure if it was the wind or something else. Val, Scarlet and Ray were standing outside of the mouth of the cave. Zyler seemed to be captivated by something in the distance.

Ray ran up to her the moment he saw her. All Cora wanted to do was jump into his arms and she didn't care who was watching. After her last encounter with Prince Lyon she knew for certain she had feelings for Ray.

Once he was only a few steps away she tackled him to the ground. They both landed in a pile of fresh snow. Cora had landed on top of him their lips were only a few centimeters apart. She felt his warm breath on her face.

"My apologies," he tucked a strand of her long blonde hair behind her ear. "Lily never did anything like this and I'm not sure how to react."

"Just be yourself,"

Their fingers tightly intertwined.

Val loudly cleared her throat. Her cheeks blushed slightly pink. She was clearly uncomfortable.

Scarlet on the other hand seemed to be enjoying the spectacle.

The pair quickly got up and shook the snow off their clothes.

Val opened her notebook and began skimming the pages. "I put together a strategy to help us inject all of the Tibicenas with the antidote. Can someone go get Zyler so I can explain the plan to everyone?"

Cora regained her composure. "I'll go get him."

Zyler sat on a rocky ledge on the side of the mountain watching the sun rise.

Cora sat beside him but he refused to look away.

The view was truly breathtaking. The entire sky was painted painted vibrant shades of pink and orange. There were stretches of snow covered trees for as far as the eye could see.

Zyler was the first to break the silence. "You know they say that the sunrises on Mt. Nevado are some of the most beautiful in the world? I never thought I'd see one with my own eyes though."

Cora wasn't used to Zyler being so serious. "Why not?"

"I grew up in a crowded orphanage in western Thessionia. I had nothing not even a name. There wasn't enough food to go around. I was sure I was going to die there. One day a family decided to adopt me. Neither of them made it into the Prestige Program so they didn't have much money, but it was riches compared to what I was used to. They treated me like I was their own son. I made I promise that I would help them out in anyway I can. I worked days and nights in a factory so we could keep our home. My mom has always wanted to watch the sunrise on Mt. Nevado to see if it was really as beautiful as people say it is. I want to remember everything about this sunrise so I can tell her all about it."

"It's breathtaking." Cora replied.

Zyler nodded. "Maybe, if the mission goes according to plan I'll be able to take her myself with the reward money."

She had almost forgotten about the mission. "Val wants explain the plan to us."

The duo returned to the rest of the group where Scarlet was grilling Ray with questions.

"How long have you and Cora been together?"

"We met about a week ago and we've hardly been apart since then."

"I can't believe Cora has a boyfriend and a cute one too!"

"It's not that surprising." Cora grumbled. She had gone on a few dates in high school but never a serious relationship. Warrior training always came first. Ray wasn't even technically her boyfriend.

"You shouldn't be surprised. Coraline is a lovely lady. Anyone would be lucky to have someone like her." Ray said.

Cora's heart fluttered upon hearing his complement.

"Now that everyone is here I'll explain our plan. Zyler made us flashlights so we'll be able to see inside the cave. Scarlet has created an antidote. They won't hurt her, it's our job to hold them off long enough for her to inject them. Zyler and I created these stub collars they will immobilize the Tibicenas without harming them. We have no idea what's waiting for us inside so it's important to proceed with extreme caution," Val said.

Zyler handed out the flashlights and collars.

The group stared into the darkness. Each person to afraid to take the first step.

Scarlet ended up being the first one to enter the cave. She motioned for the rest of the group to follow her.

They walked through the icy caverns. It was dead silent.

Ray tightly squeezed Cora's hand.

A several pairs of eyes gazed at them trough the blackness.

They let out a loud growl which made Cora's heart nearly burst with fear. She didn't hesitate to jump in front of her friends ready to defend them.

There in front of her stood the most frightening creature she'd ever seen. It towered over her. It had black fur that blended into the darkness and two eyes the color of fresh blood. It's fangs were sharper than her sword. This was the Alpha.

It mauled at her chest but she sliced open

it's neck with her sword.

The Alpha grabbed her by her injured shoulder with its teeth. She tried to fight back. It threw her head first into the ice wall.

Her mouth filled up with blood and she could feel her consciousness fading away.

14

— · —

CHAPTER 14

An awful smell entered her nose which made her gag. She shined her flashlight around the cave looking for where it was coming from. Cora almost screamed. Right in front of her stood a rotten corpse. She tried her hardest to calm herself down. She took a step closer. The corpse was wearing the royal crest on it's sleeve. It had a bejeweled sword tucked away in in it's sheath. Cora grabbed it even though she had promised herself she would never steal a sword again. The darkness made it difficult to see but, the sword looked extremely expensive.

The sound of angry growls echoed throughout the cave. Her head spun around and around. She leaned up against the frozen wall to try to gain stability. She wandered through to lonely caverns. She tried to follow the sounds but they were difficult to hear over the ringing in her ears.

Several pairs of glowing eyes surrounded her. She blinked rapidly to make sure she wasn't hallucinating.

They bared their teeth and jump towards her. She tried to defend herself. For some reason her sword felt much heavier.

One of them knocked the flashlight out of her hand. It became lost in the black. She couldn't see anything. She slashed through darkness hoping to hit something but she didn't. She tried to run away but she slipped and fell on the ice.

The sound of claws scraping against the ice rapidly approached her. She tried as hard as she could to get up. Blood poured out of her nose and mouth. Her muscles ached. No matter how hard she tried she couldn't stand. This is how it ends.

The pack was getting closer and closer then they stopped. Why did they stop? Someone stood in front of her.

"Stay back Coraline." He had no weapon but he was ready to defend her with his life.

"Ray, take this," she handed him the stolen sword.

He took it from her hand. "Thank you."

One Tibicena jumped out of nowhere and bit Ray's leg. It cracked its teeth on the metal which gave Ray enough time to put a collar on.

She faded in and out of consciousness. She heard several sounds that she couldn't distinguish.

"Don't worry Cora we've got this." Was that Val?

Various voices mixed with the sounds of swords clashing and angry howls bounced off the walls. Her friends had come to her aid. She wanted to fight beside them so badly. She tried to see the fight, but it was too dark.

A pair of yellow eyes stared down at the commotion. He quite enjoyed the sight of bloodshed. From the look of it he appeared to be winning. The girl would break eventually. Once the Blood King was dead he could finally sleep at night knowing justice has been served. Tibicenas surrounded the group. It really was a shame so many people needed to die but the ends justified the means.

Violent barks came from every direction. Cora finally managed to stand but her bones ached. There was about thirty of them. There was no way they could take them all on. Cora scoured the cave looking for anything that could get them out of this situation. The icicles!

"Val hit the icicles!" Cora cried out.

Val threw a shock grenade at the icicles. The impact was enough to send them raining down.

One slammed Cora in the head causing her to once again lose consciousness.

She woke up in the doctor's hut with her head wrapped in bandages.

Ray sat fast asleep in a chair in the corner of the room. His right arm was tightly bandaged and his face was covered with scratches. His metal leg had been ripped to shreds. Her heart broke. She was barely any help during the fight. She couldn't even protect Ray. Maybe she wasn't cut out for this.

The doctor entered the room and her puppy scampered behind her. She grinned when she realized Cora was awake.

"You know, he stayed with you all night." She pointed to Ray. "He refused to leave your side."

Cora sat up. Her head ached.

"You've got a pretty bad concussion. It'll most likely take you a couple weeks to recover."

"How's everyone else?"

"They've only got a few scratches. They went to go claim the reward money."

Reward money? "We completed the mission?"

"Thanks to you. Your friends told me all about it. The impact held off the Tibicenas long enough for them to be given the antidote.

"But, I barely did anything.

"You made the most of your surroundings and used your instincts. I'd say you did a fine job."

Cora still had doubts but she felt reassured knowing that they had won the battle.

About half an hour later a carriage arrived to bring them down the mountain. Cora hadn't been outside since they invaded the Tibicenas' den. The sun shined brightly causing the icicles to drip. Warm weather was rare on Mt. Nevado, so it was always welcomed.

She was not going to miss trudging through the wet snow. Ray followed behind her on crutches. He was surprisingly fast considering how deep the snow was.

Val and Zyler were packing their things into the carriage. Scarlet was saying goodbye to the Tibicenas. She hugged one tightly and whispered something in it's ear. it licked her face in return. The connection between them was so strong even Cora could feel it. She could see how much it hurt Scarlet to say goodbye even though she had barely known them

.

They all piled into the carriage and it began the journey down the mountain.

"I can't believe we actually won!" Zyler exclaimed. He was right this was all way too easy. "We were like the Avengers!"

Ray placed a hand on his chin "I'm not familiar with that guild, but they must be extremely powerful if you praise them so highly."

"Is he serious?" Zyler questioned.

Cora didn't respond. The book in her hands had left her completely speechless. On this page there was a painting of the Blood King standing with a woman in a long black dress there was a look of despair in her light green eyes. Her sand colored hair was styled into intricate braids and she wore a tiara on top of her head. She looked like a queen. This must be Lily. She felt a pang of jealousy seeing Ray with another woman even though there was no feelings between them. That was not what left her speechless behind them stood a familiar shadow. The next page was covered with photographs some of them were in color and some of them were in black and white all of them had drastically different dates in the corner ranging from 1895 to 2018 but they all had one thing in common they all included a dark figure with glowing yellow eyes.

Her head spun. How was this possible? Stared at the pictures looking for some sort of clue that could help her but her efforts were fruitless and she eventually fell asleep.

The next few weeks flew by. Cora had missed a lot of training while she was recovering from her concussion so she had a lot of work to make up for. After all these weeks she still didn't have a single guild request. Ray assured her that one day a guild would be interested in her.

Tonight her parents were going out on a date so she invited her friends over to watch a movie. After much debate they decided on Captain America.

Shortly after Cora and Ray had finished getting ready, there was a knock on the door. Cora felt a twinge of anxiety in her stomach though she couldn't fathom why. She slowly opened the door and Val, Zyler and Scarlet stood outside. She let out a long sigh of relief.

"Are you going to let us in or are supposed to stand here all night?" Val asked.

"Sorry! I was afraid you were someone else." Cora said awkwardly as she let them in.

"Wow, I didn't think you were afraid of anything, Cora!" Zyler said.

Cora laughed awkwardly and tried to change the subject. "Where's Dimitri tonight?"

"He's with the guild. It's all he ever does anymore." Scarlet rolled her eyes but you could see a hint of sadness in her face.

Cora had hardly seen Dimitri since she returned from Mt. Nevado. They were both so busy now. "I'm really glad you came, Scarlet."

A small smile crept across her lips.

Val sat a large box on the table.

"What's that?" Cora asked.

"It's a little gift Zyler and I put together for Ray," she replied.

"What is the occasion?" Ray asked admiring the box.

"We felt bad about your leg," Zyler said gesturing to the void where Ray's right leg should be.

"Don't worry, it was extremely uncomfortable." Ray said.

"That's why we made you this." Val opened the box revealing a sleek black prosthetic. "It's only a prototype but it should help you move a lot easier and feel more comfortable."

His eyes lit up. "Thank you. Very few people have been this kind to me."

"It sounds like you need better friends." Zyler interjected.

The group settled in and watched the movie. About halfway through the movie a loud noise sounded from the kitchen. Cora got up to go see what could have made it but she couldn't find anything so she sat back down.

A shadow materialized out of the darkness. "I've come for the Blood King!"

Ray stood up and pulled out his sword. "It appears you've found him."

15

CHAPTER 15

R ay stood up and pulled out his sword. "It appears you've found him."

The shadow's eyes lit up with recognition. "Today is the day you pay for your sins."

Ray took a step closer to the shadow. "I challenge you to a duel if I win you will leave and never come back here," Ray looked at Cora for a long time like it may be the last time he'll ever see her. "And if you win you may do whatever you want with me."

"I agree to a duel, but if anyone is to interfere I will kill everyone in this room." He glared at Cora.

The two kings shook hands then took fighting stances.

"I hope you're prepared to die, Blood King."

"Hit me with your best shot."

The shadow took a stab at Ray's chest but he easily deflected it.

He took another stab at the throat this time. Ray slashed through his hand causing him to drop the sword. Blood poured out of the wound. The yellow in his eyes began to fade away.

Ray ran his sword across the shadow's neck. His red eyes lit up with amusement. "I can't believe after all these years you still manage to lose to me, old friend."

"I am not your friend! I am the King of Shadows!"

Ray laughed. "Please, you are no a king. You may have every-one else fooled but I can see right through you."

"You know nothing about me or my power!" He pulled a vile of black liquid out of his pocket and drank it before Ray had time to react.

The color returned to his eyes and his body became one with the shadows. He disappeared into the darkness. Ray quickly spun around looking for him.

The shadow plunged a dagger into Ray's back causing him to cry out in pain. Cora watched from the sidelines in horror. He was going to kill Ray and there was nothing she could do. She never would have thought she would ever be rooting for the Blood King much less be devastated by the thought of losing him. Everyone was wrong about him. He was more than just some killer but no one would ever know the truth.

Ray collapsed onto the floor. No one made a sound.

The shadow crept close to Ray. "Burn in Hell, Blood King!"

"I'll meet you there!" Ray pierced through the shadow's chest. He gripped the wounded area tightly and stumbled back in pain. "This isn't the end! The Armageddon has only just begun!" He disappeared into the night without a trace.

Val cleaned out the wound on Ray's back then began stitching it up. He winced in pain. Cora squeezed his hand so tight she feared she might break it. "Don't worry, Coraline. I've had far worse injuries than this."

Cora believed him. Almost every inch of his sleek yet well defined torso was covered in battle scars.

Zyler paced back and forth in front of the tv. "So, let me get this straight you're the Blood King?"

"Yes."

"I don't believe it!"

Cora stood to her feet. "I it sounds crazy but-"

"I can't believe you actually believe this! Do you believe him, Val?"

Val didn't look up from her work. "It's not plausible. The Blood King died roughly 2,000 years ago."

"Thank you! Finally someone acknowledges this is crazy!"

"I think we should hear him out," Scarlet murmured. This was the first time she had spoken since the shadow attacked. "I know it sounds crazy, but there's no harm in hearing what he has to say."

"I'll be more than happy to answer all of your questions," Ray reassured him.

Zyler crossed his arms and sighed. "Alright, I'll listen."

"I grew up in an estate right here in Silvershore. My mother didn't want me to grow up in the palace so she raised me there. I didn't have any friends I was taught to never trust anyone.

One day the son of a couple of traveling magicians tried to steal food from the estate. His name was Galen Rivero. Instead of turning him in I decided to let him go free under the condition he'd play with me when he was in town. I used to sneak him into the estate he would always end up stealing something. He was a pain but he was closest thing to a friend ever knew. After my father was killed I moved into the palace where I was crowned king. Rivero begged to come with me and I was stupid enough to let him. I was forced into an arranged marriage with a young duchess. On our wedding day she said she wanted me dead. I wish I had taken her words more seriously. I became obsessed with ruling,. I was going to make Thessionia the greatest empire the world had ever seen. I conquered all of the surrounding nations. I told myself I was doing them a favor, they lacked strong leadership but deep down I knew I was doing the wrong thing. People stared calling me the Blood King, I hated that name. Rivero stopped speaking to me all together. I had heard rumors that someone inside the palace was planning to assasinate me. I knew Rivero was behind it from the start but didn't want to believe it. One night when Lily and I returned to our room the royal guard ambushed me. Rivero was also there. Apparently, the two of them had been planning my demise for months. I never really knew why they did it. I didn't fight back. Everyone hated me and no one was going to mourn my passing. They didn't want to leave any evidence behind so they decided the best way to dispose of me was to trap me alive in burial crystals and move me to a secret location. Lily showed no emotion as she killed me. 2,000 years later I woke up confused in Coraline's home. She's been helping me fit in here. I don't know how I survived for so long nor why I awoke when I did, but I hope we can continue to be friends."

Everyone just sat in silence trying to comprehend that much information. It was becoming unbearably awkward. Then Val spoke. "How are you so young?"

"I believe the burial persevered my youth."

"I mean I never knew the Blood King was so young I always thought the Blood King was a creepy old guy."

Ray let out a faint laugh. "People have said a lot of things about me some of them are true but most are exaggerations."

Zyler still stood with eyes wide in surprise. "You're the real deal aren't you?"

"Yes, I am."

"Do you know who attacked us?" Scarlet asked.

"I have an idea but I'm not completely certain yet."

Zyler looked at Cora. "Why didn't you tell us?"

"Because he's not as bad as everyone thinks he is and I didn't want you to have the wrong impression of him. Plus none of you would have believed me."

Zyler nodded. "You're right about that."

"So, what are we supposed to do now?" Val asked.

"I don't know." Cora said defeated.

Cora left the group and went to her room to fetch the book hopefully it would be able to help them but her book wasn't on the bed where she left it. She frantically scoured the room looking for it. Then she saw it on the top shelf in her closet. How did it get up there?

As she went to grab it she felt something cold wrap itself around her body. It covered her mouth before she could cry for help. She reached for the book but something stabbed into her arm. She couldn't breathe. Her fingers grazed her sword. She had to grab it. It's grip got stronger. It felt like her insides were being crushed. Something sharp ripped through her clothes. She reached for her sword one more time. She strained to reach it. It was just centimeters away from her hand. She just had to reach a little further.

16

CHAPTER 16

"Cora," a voice called out to her. It was so familiar yet it had begun to leave her memory.

"Grandmother?"

The book glowed a bright shade of blue.

"No matter what happens you mustn't let the darkness control you."

Cora stretched her hand desperately trying to reach the sword tucked away in her sheath. Something sharp pricked her palm but she didn't flinch. Her fingers wrapped around the sword. In one swift motion she whipped out her sword and severed the bondage that was holding her.

Her cuts stung but that didn't matter. The book had spoken to her. How?

She flipped on the light switch. Severed vines were scattered all over the floor. They were a deep black color with sharp purple thorns, some of them were stained red with her blood. There was no doubt about it, these were the same vines from Mt. Nevado. But they didn't grow in Silvershore.

The book lay on the floor opened to a page somewhere in the middle. It had stopped glowing.

She tiptoed around the decapitated vines, afraid of injuring herself further.

She gently picked up the book off the floor, then sat on her bed.

Surprisingly, the page she was currently looking at had detailed drawings of the vines. Below them was another letter.

Dear Cora, I hope you are still fighting the best you can. If you're reading this, then the darkness has already begun to spread. Soon it will overrun all of Thessionia. The King of Shadows will return on Blood King's Day. You must defeat him then. I know I'm asking a lot of you and I wish things were simpler but I have faith you will succeed.

Blood King's Day was only a week away. How was she going to be ready to face him by then?

When she arrived downstairs everyone except Ray were gone.

"Where is everyone?" She asked.

"They decided it was best that they head home. It's been an eventful night."

"Oh."

"They wanted to say goodbye to you but, you took so long upstairs."

"About that," Cora quickly glanced around the room to make sure no one was watching, then opened the book. "The King of Shadows is going to return soon."

His eyes widened with surprise. "When?"

"On Blood King's day."

Ray looked away. "What's that?"

Cora was unsure of the best way to explain it to him. "Well, it's a Thessionian holiday where we celebrate the anniversary of the death of the Blood King." Knowing what she knows now, Cora felt bad she had celebrated it all these years.

Ray didn't say anything.

Cora started to ramble. "It's kind of a huge deal around here. Don't take it personally."

'Why would I take it personally?"

"Because...you're..." she fumbled over her words. "You aren't upset?"

"Of course I'm not upset. The Blood King is dead. As far as anyone else is concerned i'm an ordinary civilian named Ray Castillo. The Blood King will remain a piece of history and nothing more."

Cora didn't know what to say so she said nothing. Ray placed his hand on top of hers which made her heart flutter.

"When is it?"

"When is what?" Cora was so flustered she had completely forgotten what they were talking about. Cora could no longer deny it. She had feelings for Ray, but they had more important matters to attend to right now.

"Blood Kings Day," Ray clarified.

"Next Sunday, so we'll have about a week to prepare."

"Do we have any idea what he's planning?"

"No."

"There's not much we can do, then."

"We need to stop him!" Cora protested.

"If we don't know what he's planning than we have no idea how to stop it."

Cora wanted to argue, but he was right. All she knew was that darkness was spreading, bringing chaos with it. He was going to return on Blood King's day and she needed to stop him.

Ray stood up "It's getting quite late."

It was late and Cora felt guilty because of how badly she wanted to sleep right now. She should probably be plotting how to stop the King of Shadows, but Ray was right there wasn't much they could do.

"Good night," He whispered in her ear. They're lips were barely a centimeter apart. She wanted to kiss him so badly but she resisted.

Instead she wrapped her hands around his neck. "Good night, Ray."

The next day moved at a snail's place. For some reason most of her class didn't show up to training today. Since she had missed so much training between her trip up Mt. Nevado and recovering from her concussion she had fallen considerably behind and had a hard time keeping up with the others.

After a long day of training Cora wandered through the castle corridors. Several students holding large boxes of decorations were scattered throughout the halls. They must be preparing for the Blood King's Day celebrations. She didn't think anyone would mind if she took a sneak peek at the decorations in the ballroom. She crept around the corner and into the ballroom.

She was so distracted she bumped into the someone on her way in. Cora was startled by the sound of birds squawking.

"Hey, it's alright. Calm down." Scarlet eased the birds until they were quiet. There were many brightly colored birds throughout the room. Cora wasn't sure what type of birds they were but, they looked exotic.

"What are you doing here?" Cora asked.

"I'm on the party planning committee."

"I didn't know that."

Scarlet laughed. "Do you know anything about me?"

"I wish I knew more," Cora confessed.

Scarlet shyly peered through her hair. The pair stood in silence for a few moments before Cora spoke. "I really like your birds."

Scarlet's eyes lit up with excitement. "They helped me with the decorations," she stepped aside revealing a fully decorated ballroom. The entire room was lit up by candlelight. Blood red colored drapes hung from the ceiling. Black shields with red lions painted on them hung on the walls. The tables were decorated with bouquets of red roses. Something about about the room felt magical. "They were the ones that hung the drapes from the ceiling," Scarlet continued.

Cora stared at the ballroom in awe. Something about almost felt familiar to her though she wasn't sure why. "Everything looks so beautiful!" Cora exclaimed.

Scarlet tried her hardest not to blush but she couldn't hide her satisfaction. "Ray helped me with the design. I wanted it to look as authentic as possible."

Jealously struck Cora like an arrow through the heart. She hated the fact that she was jealous over something so trivial. She used to look down on people for getting upset over boys but she understood now. It was stupid and she knew it was just because Ray and Scarlet have been talking that doesn't mean anything has happened between them. So Cora set aside her feelings and continued to admire the room when something out the window caught her eye. Black clouds with purple lightning filled the horizon.

Scarlet turned around to see what had caught Cora's attention. Scarlet gently pet one of the birds. "The animals can usually predict when a storm is coming. I noticed they were acting especially strange this morning then those clouds appeared out of nowhere. I'm starting to worry."

Cora clenched her fists. This was the Armageddon. Soon all of Thessionia will be overrun and there was nothing she could do. Her thoughts were interrupted by the sound of two sets of footsteps.

Dimitri poked his head into the ballroom. "Hey Scar, are you ready to go?"

"I told you not to call me that," she mumbled.

"What?" Dimitri hollered from across the room.

Scarlet let out an exasperated sigh. "I'm ready."

Cora was surprised by who followed. Prince Lyon limped behind on crutches. His eyes widened when he caught glimpse of the fully decorated room. "I've been to more Blood King's Day balls than I can count, but none have ever looked as authentic as this one. You've done an excellent job."

Scarlet could no longer stop herself from blushing. "Thank you, Your Highness."

Prince Lyon turned to Dimitri. "I hope you'll keep in touch about my offer."

The pair shook hands. "Of course," Dimitri tried his hardest to mask the nervousness in his voice but it was obvious his conversation with the prince had left him starstruck.

Prince Lyon inched his way towards Cora.

Cora was unsure of what to say to him. During their previous interactions she was always so dazed, but now she felt nothing. She tried to come up with something to say. "Fancy meeting you here," was the best she could come up with.

He gently kissed her hand. "Actually I was looking for you," he replied.

"You were?" She stuttered.

He squeezed her hands. "I need to speak with you alone."

Before she could respond he dragged her down the hallway and into anther room leaving Scarlet and Dimitri behind.

This room was so long it seemed to stretch on forever. The walls were covered with paintings of nobles all of which had the same scarlet colored hair as Lyon.

They sat down on a bench in front of a painting of two small boys with long red hair. One of the boys looked familiar.

The pair sat in silence for what felt like an eternity. Cora wondered why Prince Lyon would possibly to need to speak with her alone.

He tightly squeezed her hand which made her flinch. Was Prince Lyon in love with her? "Your Highness_" She began but was cut off.

He placed a finger on her lips silencing her. "There's no need to be so formal."

He tried to wrap an arm around her but she pulled away. "Listen, I really don't feel comfortable with this."

He let go of her. "My apologies, I didn't mean to make you uncomfortable." He turned to his bodyguard. "Why don't you go get us some tea."

"But, Your Highness," he protested.

Lyon locked eyes with the guard for a long time before the guard begrudgingly exited the room muttering something incoherent.

Lyon let out a long sigh. "I thought he'd never leave," He stood up. "Now I can tell you the real reason I called you here. I trust you'll keep this confidential."

The blonde slowly nodded.

He gently ran his fingers down the side of the painting. Do you remember the day my brother, Prince Liam was killed?"

She shook her head. She was too young to remember the day it happened but her parents or the news would occasionally bring up the tragedy of the the two year old prince that was murdered in cold blood but it wasn't talked about often.

"I remember it perfectly. I was out playing in the courtyard and then a group of palace servants came to tell me the news. They kept apologizing to me but no words could fix the damage that had been done, I lost my best friend that day. Father didn't eat or sleep for weeks after the incident. He hasn't been the same since."Tears welled up in his eyes. "I've come to the conclusion that the royal guard is incompetent."

Cora was speechless. She had learned so much new information and she had so many questions. "But, the royal guard, they caught the killer right?" She stuttered.

Prince Lyon shook his head. "They executed the wrong man and then covered it up," He banged his fists against the wall. He took a deep breath and regained his composure then continued. "Which is why I'm putting together a team of the best warriors I can find to protect me from these kinds of threats." He handed her a business card. "Think about it."

Cora walked down the hallways all alone. Everyone else had left awhile ago. She was tired and her throat felt dry. She never did get that tea. She turned down a corridor heading towards the exit when she saw the dead body of Prince Lyon's bodyguard with the words.

TIME IS RUNNING OUT!

Written in blood.

17

CHAPTER 17

She was startled by a knock on her door. Her heart pounded so loudly she thought it might burst. She tightly gripped her sword, afraid of what she might find on the other side, she slowly opened the door to see her father standing on the other side. She dropped her sword and let out a sigh of relief. "Oh thank God it's you!"

"Who else would it be? The Blood King?" he laughed.

Cora forced out a laugh.

He handed her a mug full of apple cider, a traditional Blood King's Day beverage. "I'm here to wish you a happy Blood King's Day."

She gladly accepted the mug and took a sip. The fresh, tangy flavor warmed her tastebuds.

"I also wanted to check on you. You've been really out of it lately. I want to make sure you're okay."

"Why wouldn't I be?" Cora could think of many reasons why she wouldn't be okay, but he didn't know about any of them.

He picked up the business card off the desk. "I know about your offer."

"How?" Cora asked bewildered.

He reached into his pocket and pulled out a business card almost identical to the one she had received. "This isn't the first time the royal family has tried something like this. King Lucien tried something very similar sixteen years ago," He stared blankly out the window to ashamed to let his daughter see how weak he was.

"I'm guessing it didn't go well."

He gently shut the laptop on her desk unable to bear the sight of the article. "The royal family hired the Ironheart guild as personal security on a diplomatic mission to the outer reaches of Thessionia. My partner and I were put in charge of protecting Prince Liam. Unlike everyone else, we were put on the back of the train, they thought it would be safer there. An assassin snuck aboard and detached our car from the rest of the train leaving us stuck in the middle of nowhere alone. He was a man dressed in all black with bright yellow eyes. His face was completely covered so I couldn't see what he looked like but that didn't make him any less intimidating. He demanded we turn the prince over to him, we refused, which made him furious. He easily took on both of us at the same time. We used every trick in the book, but he was too powerful." He ran his hand down his injured spine. "I fought until I couldn't stand anymore. He took the prince and disappeared into the blackness. A few weeks later Prince Liam was confirmed as dead. My partner vouched for me so my punishment wasn't as severe as it could have been but, we were both discharged from the guild. I failed my mission and now I have to face the guilt and shame every single day." He turned to her. "I want you to take this decision seriously."

"Why didn't you tell me about this sooner?" she asked him.

"You've always seen me as some kind of hero and I was ashamed to tell you the truth."

"You did everything you could to protect Prince Liam, Dad. You fought until you couldn't stand anymore. You'll always be a hero in my book."

The two warriors sat in silence for a few minutes.

Cora checked her watch. "I'm not meeting up with my friends until noon. Why don't you help me with my training?"

A smile of pure joy spread across his lips. She hadn't seen her father smile like that in a long time. So the pair trained together until they were both worn out.

Cora went into her room to change out of her sweaty clothes when the book began to glow again. She was so startled she dropped the clothes she was holding. The pages seemed to turn themselves until she reached a page near the end of the book.

Dear Cora, I have faith today is the day you will defeat the King of Shadows. I know you're probably frightened, but you should know the King of Shadows has no power of his own, his power comes from potions and trickery. He has limited combat abilities, remember that. Your enemy underestimates you, but you are stronger than he will ever be. You have found a very powerful ally in the Blood King, you will be excellent companions to each other. I can't express how desperately I wish I could be here today to help you. Thessionia is falling into chaos, Prince Lyon is dead, but there is another heir to the throne and they will become one of the greatest rulers Thessionia has ever seen. I know you will win this war.

Cora didn't know how to process her emotions. Prince Lyon was dead? How could this happen? This must be a mistake! She slammed the book shut.

Laughter filled the crowed streets. Everyone was so excited for the holiday. The sent of warm cider and meat being grilled over an open flame filled her nostrils. The trees were decorated with paper lanterns and bright red ribbons. Several people in the crowd wore brightly colored costumes, some even dressed as the Blood King and let out cartoonishly evil laughs, which almost made her giggle. If only they knew the real Blood King. A wave of sadness crashed over her, she used to love Blood King's Day, but this year she had too much on her mind.

Was Prince Lyon really dead?

She was greeted by her friends who were seated seated around a picnic table. Each of them looked distraught. Cora forced a smile and sat beside Ray. Directly across from them sat Scarlet who was looking especially distressed.

"Are you nervous about tonight?" Cora asked her.

"No...yes, I mean," She stuttered over her words. "I am nervous but that's not the only thing on my mind,"

Cora was afraid of what else could possibly happen.

"Dimitri went out last night he couldn't say where, apparently it's 'top secret' we haven't seen him since. He's probably just at a friends house or something." Scarlet said, her voice full of uncertainty.

Cora looked up at towards the heavens, the dark clouds almost covered the entire sky. A loud crash of thunder sounded in the distance. This was no coincidence.

"Don't worry, I promise I'll find him." Cora reassured her friend.

Val stood up. "Now that everyone's here we can explain our plan. If Cora's book is correct then The King of Shadows will attack tonight. We have to be ready for whatever tricks he might have up his sleeves." She held up a small device in her hand. "Zyler and I created these communication devices so we'll be able to keep in touch. Just place them in your ear and we'll be able to communicate over long distances." She pointed to a red button on the side of the device. "Press this button and it will send out a distress signal I've equipped a tracking device so we'll be able to find you. Remember to only press the button in a

real

emergency." Val scowled at Zyler.

"Hey! Running out of toilet paper is a really emergency, Val!" Zyler protested.

Val rolled her eyes. "Scarlet brewed an anti potion that should neutralize his powers when injected."

Scarlet pulled a syringe full of white liquid out of her pocket. "It is a very difficult potion to make this was all I had time to brew. We'll only have one shot at this. I'm sorry I couldn't do more."

Zyler squeezed her shoulders. "Are you kidding? I don't know anyone else that can make complex potions. We might actually have a chance at defeating this guy and if the potion doesn't work then you can summon an animal army to stop him."

She let out a faint chuckle.

Cora eyes drifted over to Ray, he sat in silence stuffing his face with Doritos. It wasn't unusual for him to be quiet during group meetings but something felt wrong.

The meeting went on for about an hour. Planning for the attack proved difficult since they had no idea what he was q planning. Cora's tenacity began to dwindle. She questioned if it was even possible to defeat him for good or would he haunt them forever. All she knew was after today things wouldn't be the same. Ray didn't say a single word the entire meeting. As soon as it ended she pulled him aside to speak to him in private. "Do you wanna talk about what's bothering you?"

"Trust me Coraline, I'm doing perfectly fine," he said as he ate another handful of chips.

"You're stress eating,"

"I am not!" He began to protest, but stopped himself. He set down the bag of chips, then pulled her into a warm embrace. "I don't want to fight anymore." He whispered, his voice sounded so broken, like someone who had seen too many battles for someone his age. "I promise I'll always be here support you, but I never want to hurt anyone ever again."

"I'd never ask you to do something you didn't feel comfortable doing and if you'd rather stand on the sidelines than fight, I'm okay with that." Cora gently rubbed his back, she could feel deep battle scars through his shirt. It never really occurred to her how many times his life must have been in grave danger. The realization hit her like a ton of bricks. This could be their last day together. Of course she knew the mission was dangerous, deadly even, but she had been in denial that this could very well be the end. This could be her last chance to tell him how she felt. Her heart sped up at the very thought of declaring her affections, but it was now or never. She took a deep breath. "Please go out with with me?" She squeaked.

"What?"

Cora cleared her throat. "I want you to go out on a date with me today." She said with much more confidence this time.

He stared at her lips for a few moments than kissed her hand. "It would be an honor to go out with you."

She took him by the hand and pulled him into the middle of the festivities. They spent the afternoon exploring the different stands that had been set up for the celebration. One of them was filled with plastic swords and toy Tibicenas, another sold chains made out of pearls, but by far Cora's favorite stand was the one that sold cotton candy. Once the sun went down the couple sat on a hill away from the crowds but close enough to see the street below.

"Do you really celebrate the Blood King's death with rainbow explosions?"

Cora laughed as she took a bite of her cotton candy. "Yes, they're called fireworks."

"That sounds dangerous."

"It's what the Blood King would have wanted," Cora joked.

He raised his eyebrows playfully.

Cora rested her head on his shoulder. "No matter what happens tonight, I want you to I'm really glad I busted you out of those crystals."

He lifted her head so their eyes met. "I am too. For the first time in my life I'm happy to be alive and it's all thanks to you."

She moved in even closer to him and wrapped her arms around his neck.

"I was wondering...I mean...never mind." He stuttered. In his eyes like there was something he wanted to ask so desperately, but couldn't bring himself to say it.

"I really want to hear what you were going to ask me."

"Would it be appropriate for me to kiss you?"

Without another word Cora's lips crashed into his. Ray sat stunned for a moment before giving in to the sweet taste of her watermelon flavored chapstick. She tangled her fingers into his short black hair. For one moment everything felt perfect.

No one had predicted there would be a thunderstorm today. There was supposed to be nothing but sunshine and warmth. All the vendors hurried to pack up their things before the rain ruined them. Bright streaks of purple lightning lit up the black horizon. Cora and Ray ran through the streets looking for shelter to keep them dry. Through all the commotion Cora caught sight of someone familiar. Prince Lyon! Cora releases her grip on Ray's hand and followed after him.

18

CHAPTER 18

"**L**yon!" Cora cried out.

His pace quickened upon hearing his name.

Cora sped up desperate to catch up to him.

He darted down a dark alleyway and Cora followed.

After what felt like a labyrinth of twists and turns she finally caught up to him.

He leaned up against the wall gasping for air "Prince Lyon!" Cora cried out as she ran over to help him.

"You shouldn't have followed me her he snapped!"

Before she could question why heavy footsteps approached from behind her. She turned to see... Dimitri? He grabbed her by the neck and forced her into a sleeper hold. She tried to pry his arms off of her but her attempts were fruitless.

She woke up seated at a long banquet table. The only light in the room was the faint glowing of the fireplace.

"Sleeping Beauty is finally awake." Prince Lyon stood by the fire holding an open book in his hands.

"What happened to Dimitri?" Cora asked though she was afraid to hear the answer "Don't worry, I took care of him you'll never have to worry about him again."

Why would Dimitri try to hurt her? They hadn't talked much recently but how could someone change so much so fast? She needed answers. She tried to stand but then she realized her hands and feet were tied to the chair.

"Untie me," she said, her voice was firm and demanding.

"Calm down. There's nothing to worry about," he walked towards her and picked up a goblet off the table. "You look thirsty you should have a drink." He placed the goblet on her lips. It was filled with a bright pink liquid. The scent was vaguely familiar to her. The taste was sweet and warm, it was intoxicating ,the more she drank the more she wanted. Her tastebuds were overwhelmed by the flavor of cherries.

In an instant everything made sense. She spat out the the drink back into the chalice. "You've been using a love potion on me!"

"Where would you get a ridiculous idea like that?" Prince Lyon laughed, but you could hear a twinge if nervousness in his voice.

"You've been putting it in the tea the whole time, haven't you? You've been trying to seduce me!"

He threw the goblet against the wall in a brief moment of rage. His eyes flickered a shade of yellow. "You didn't respond to my threats so I had to make you talk a different way."

Prince Lyon was the King of Shadows? Didn't the King of Shadows attack him on Mt. Nevado? Right now she needed to focus on calling backup. He had forgotten to take her earpiece, but she couldn't reach the distress button. She needed to stall for time.

She felt a steal blade brush up against her neck. "Honestly, I was hoping you'd be a good girl and I wouldn't have to kill you, but now you know too much. I should kill you now, but I'd much prefer to make the Blood King watch helplessly as you perish. You aren't the first woman I've taken away from him, but you will be the last."

Cora forced herself to put on a brave face. "Who are you?"

"I suppose there's no harm in you knowing the truth it's not like you'll live to tell the tale. My real name is Galen Rivero, but you may also know me as the King of Shadows and I'm here to make the Blood King pay for his sins."

"How are you still alive after all this time?"

"The same way the Blood King survived by incasing myself in crystals. You see, my parents where a pair of traveling magicians, but eventually they decided to settle down in Golden Crest. They tried to warn me about the Blood King, but I wanted to believe he was my friend. My parents fought in the rebellion against him, the Blood King showed them no mercy. I came up with my own plan to kill the him. Everything went according to plan. After I thought I'd killed the Blood King, some of his relatives took his remains to a secret location.

Queen Lilliana promoted me to second in command, I thought I'd finally had my revenge, but I still wasn't satisfied. I didn't sleep for a month. One night it hit me; what if, somehow, the Blood King had survived. His family refused to tell me where they were keeping him, I searched everywhere, but I had no luck. Lily tried to assure me there was no possible way for him to have survived, but I knew better. I had to know if someone could actually survive being trapped in crystals, so I started a little experiment with some of our war prisoners. To my astonishment not only can you survive being trapped, but you come out looking younger and more beautiful than you were before. The process was extremely painful. Sometimes I wished I was dead, but the results were worth it. I'd discovered how to live forever. After Lily passed away, finding the Blood King became my obsession. I hired a guild of elite warriors to search for the Blood King, but no one ever found him. I was getting old and weak. I did what I had to do to stay young. I sealed myself away and ordered my guards to wake me every thirty years. After almost two thousand years, I was ready to quit. But one day I was going through the warrior archives and found a very interesting transaction. The Bowman family had been hired to protect something large and important. The records were very secretive about what exactly it was. I convinced myself this must be the Blood King so I chased this lead and eventually it brought me here."

Cora kicked off her boots, which helped her slip her feet out of their restraints, but her hands were still bound to the chair. She caught a glimpse of a knife near the center of the table. She just had to keep him talking. "What have you done with Prince Lyon"

"Currently his corpse is rotting in a cave on top of Mt. Nevado." He chuckled to himself like he had just told a hilarious joke.

She remembered seeing the remains of someone in the Tibicenas' den. It was one of the few things she could remember about that experience. "How did you manage to take his Lyon's place without anyone noticing?"

"The palace was in a state of mourning. After the death of Prince Liam, their minds were weak, which made them susceptible to my magic. No one even noticed the difference."

"You killed Prince Liam!" Cora snapped. She slammed the table in her rage which knocked the knife on the floor.

"No, I didn't. I'm not a monster, I'm just making sure justice is served."

Cora was furious, but tried her hardest to regain her composure. "What about your guards? You killed them just to intimidate me!"

"They were planning to betray me! I did what I had to do!"

"Ray is twice the man you'll ever be."

The King of Shadows walked towards the bookshelf in the corner of the room. This was her chance! She kicked the knife up and it landed perfectly on her lap, just like she had learned in warrior training. It was finally close enough for her bound hand to reach. She cut through the rope as fast as she could, but it proved to be difficult with her hands tied. After roughly a minute of struggling her right hand was finally freed. She quickly grabbed the device out of her ear and was about to press the button.

"I wouldn't do that if I were you."

She glanced up to see the King of Shadows holding her grandmother's book over the open fireplace.

"If you press that button you'll never see this book again."

She stood completely frozen. The book was the only connection with her grandmother. What would she do without her there to guide her?

Cora closed her eyes so he couldn't see her tears. She pressed her thumb into the button as hard as she could.

He raised his eyebrows, clearly surprised by her decision. He ripped out every last page and dropped them into the flame, then threw the empty shell on floor. "You remind me of your grandmother you're stubborn just like her. Don't worry you'll be reunited with her soon."

Without hesitation she rammed her fist into his face.

He let out growl as he rubbed his cheek. "I'd love to stay, but I must get ready for the Blood King's arrival, don't worry, you'll have a friend to keep you company."

Dimitri entered the room with his sword in hand.

"I'll leave you to be reacquainted." Rivero walked out the door.

Dimitri rested the edge of his sword on her throat. "I'm so sorry, Cora."

CHAPTER 19

"Dimitri! Stop it!"

"I can't, I have to do this, The Blood King will kill all of us!"

Cora cut through the the ropes releasing her other hand.

"How could you betray me like this?" he asked her. He was visibly shaking. "I thought we were friends!"

"We are friends and I didn't betray you!" Cora answered.

"I know everything, you're working with the Blood King to destroy Prince Lyon."

He wasn't wrong, but how was she going to explain this. She took a step back and a deep breath. "The Blood King isn't the bad guy and Prince Lyon isn't who he says he is. The real prince has been dead for years, someone else has been masquerading as him using magic."

"You've officially lost your mind!"

"I know it sounds crazy..."

"You think?"

She held the knife out in front of her and slowly took another step back. "Please, I need you listen to me. Whatever Lyon told you about the Blood King is a lie. Everything we've been taught about the Blood King is a lie."

"You really have been working with him haven't you?"

The blonde nodded hesitantly.

Dimitri tucked his sword back into it's sheath. He let out a long exasperated sigh as he ran his fingers through his curls. "I don't want to hurt you, but I can't let youleave."

Cora set her knife down on the table and crossed her arms. "Fine. I'll stay here, but you should know, I have backup on the way and they won't hesitate to beat you up to get to me."

He nervously glanced out the window. Neither of them said anything for a few minutes.

"Do you remember the time when we went to the zoo and and we tried to climb into the lion cage?" Dimitri asked not making eye contact.

"We were only five!"

"You said you were going to move in with them."

Cora tried to hide her embarrassed smile. Soon her embarrassment faded into sadness. "We were so close back then."

Dimitri frowned. "Yeah, we were."

"What happened to us?"

"I guess we're drifting apart."

"I guess so."

A loud knock on the door made them both jump.

"Are you gonna answer that?" Cora leaned up against the walls and folded her arms confidently.

Dimitri's glance shifted from the door to Cora then back to the door again. He slowly approached the door with sword in hand. A faint beeping noise sounded from the other side.

With a loud crashing noise the door was reduced to splinters.

"Now that's what I call going out with a bang!" Val exclaimed as she removed her safety goggles.

Ray handed her sword to her. "Scarlet and Zyler had business they needed to take care of, they'll be joining us shortly until then we need to hold off the King of Shadows for as long as we can."

Cora smiled down at her sword this time she was ready for the final battle.

As the trio turned to exit Dimitri stood in their path with his sword pointed towards their throats. "You dragged Scarlet into this?" Anger radiated from his voice.

Ray pushed away Dimitri's sword with his own. "You have nothing to worry about, your sister is helping us out of her own free will.He glanced down at his nonexistent watch. "In fact we're supposed to be meeting her any minute now, so we should really be going."

"You're not going anywhere!"

"You've been deceived by the King of Shadows," Ray gestured to the storm clouds out the window. "He is the one responsible for this."

"You're lying." Dimitri swung his sword so quickly Ray was barely able to block it.

Ray turned to her "Coraline, I need you to go defeat the King of Shadows, I'll hold him off."

Cora nodded slowly. She knew what she needed to do. She turned back to get one last glimpse of him before running out the door with Val following behind her.

Ray slashed trough Dimitri's jacket intentionally not harming him. "I don't want to hurt you because I know how much Coraline cares about you."

Dimitri swung his sword at Ray's chest, which he instantly deflected. He swung again, this time he aimed for they face. Blocked again. He swung again and again, over and over. The room was filled with the sound of metal clashing against metal. Dimitri hardly managed to put a scratch on him he was too skilled. Before he knew it he was backed into a wall.

Ray pointed his sword between his eyes. "Surrender now or face the consequences." Ray commanded in a tone of voice he hadn't used in nearly two thousand years, a tone of voice that reminded him too much of who he used to be.

The earth below them began to quake, which caught Ray off guard long enough for Dimitri to slice open Ray's good leg.

Crimson poured out of the wound. The pain caused him to collapse onto the floor.

"Now it looks like you're the one who should surrender," Dimitri gloated.

Ray dropped his sword and raised his hands in surrender. "Congratulations, very many have challenged me and very few have been able to defeat me, you were wise to go for the legs."

Dimitri closely scanned his face. He tried his hardest not to gasp when he realized who he was speaking to. "You're the Blood King." He gripped his sword so tightly it felt like it might crumble under the pressure.

"In the flesh."

Dimitri head was filled with so many different thoughts he feared his head might explode. The real Blood King was right in front of him. He fought the Blood King and won? "You're not really what I was expecting," he thought out loud.

"I'm sorry to disappoint."

"You're just an ordinary guy."

Ray shrugged, still holding his hands up.

"I was terrified of you as a kid, I was so afraid that you were lurking in the dark corners of my room at night just waiting to strike."

Ray couldn't hold back his laughter. He laughed so hard he was nearly in tears. "Believe me I have much better things to do than hiding under your bed."

Dimitri grumbled something foul under his breath then re-gained his composure. "My point is everyone is so scared of you, but here you are, my prisoner, you're completely defense-less,"

"Oh, but I'm not defenseless, I could easily snap your neck right now, but it would break Coraline's heart and I've been trying not to kill people anymore. I could escape if I wanted to the only reason I'm still here is because I want to be."

Dimitri starred him down trying to determine if he was bluff-ing or not to no avail. "If you can leave then why are you choosing to stay?"

"Coraline is in the fight of her life against the King of Shadows and the last thing she needs is your interference, I'm here to distract you."

The earth shook again. This time lighting struck the top of the castle short circuiting the power.

"Why are you telling me this?"

"Because it's time for you to decide who you are and who's side you're on. We can fight together as brothers to defeat this foe or you can stand with the King of Shadows, who thinks of you as nothing more than a puppet and be forced to fight against me and your best friend. You can stand with me or get out of my way, what will it be?"

20

CHAPTER 20

After an eternity of wandering she tripped down a medium sized staircase and fell on her knees. She promptly stood back up. Her legs ached from the fall, they were most likely going to bruise in the following weeks, if she lived that long.

"Snap out of it!" She whispered to herself. "I'm not going to die!" She had to stay positive. She had to survive, for her parents and for Ray. She continued to brush her fingers against the cobblestone walls until she felt something wooden in front of her, a door. She slowly pushed it open just a crack. She peered through the opening, the door lead to an outdoor arena.

The King of Shadows stood in the center wearing a dark cloak holding a bottle filled with a smoky black liquid in hand. He promptly gulped down the entire bottle which caused his green eyes to turn yellow. He stepped out of her line of vision. She gradually pushed the door open hoping to catch him by surprise. The hinges creaked loudly, the sound echoed throughout the entire arena. He turned to face her, his beady eyes ripped right through her soul then he disappeared.

She felt him grab her from behind and place a hand over her mouth, it was all far too familiar to her. She was prepared this time, she wasn't going to let him intimidate her ever again. She quickly spun around, pulled out her sword and jabbed it straight through his heart.

"It has taken me two thousand years to perfect my potion." Her sword fazed right through him. Her attack didn't injure him at all. "I've finally done it, nothing can harm me now." He forcibly grabbed her by the wrists and vanished taking her with him.

For a few brief moments it felt like she was drowning in a sea of shadows. The darkness felt like it would consume her entirely. Before she could comprehend what was happening she was transported to the center of the arena. The pouring rain instantly soaked through her clothes and caused her to shiver.

The King of Shadows pushed her to the ground. Her mouth was filled with the taste of mud. Her knees throbbed from the impact, but she forced herself to get back up.

He pulled two swords out of his sleeves. He swung them directly towards her face, she held her sword to block his attack, but he continued to grind his swords into hers. She pushed back as hard as she could.

"You know, very few people have managed to surprise me. I underestimated you, that was my mistake, one I'll never make again."

Cora swiftly maneuvered herself out of his grasp causing him to stumble. He regained his balance then disappeared. He reappeared behind her. She swung and missed. He appeared to her left then to her right she missed both times. He popped up from a million different directions. She could barely keep up with his attacks and he showed no sign of slowing down. He had managed to leave several scratches on her, but she refused to let him know the pain they caused her.

He materialized a few feet away from her. "You remind me of your grandmother, she also fought me until her dying breath. She wasn't strong enough to defeat me and neither are you."

Her insides boiled with rage. Without thinking she charged towards him. He vanished then emerged from the darkness behind her. He forced her to the ground once more. She tried to get back up, but her aching muscles would not allow her to do so.

He kicked her in the face with his steel toed boot. "Pathetic." He remarked under his breath. Blood poured out of her nostrils. When he wasn't looking she slipped her hand into her pocket, the potion antidote was still in tact. She just had to get close enough to inject it. She desperately wished her friends were here to back her up, but for now she had to she had to face him alone.

As she crept towards him she noticed his movements were slowing down and his eyes were beginning to lose their color. He was distracted by some in the distance. This was her chance to strike! His shoulder was within her grasp. She reached out to insert the injection. Before she had time to think he spun around and carved a deep gash into the palm of her hand causing her to drop the antidote. The wound throbbed so hard she couldn't help but let out a cry in anguish.

"Did you really think I wouldn't see that coming?" He scoffed.

"Stop this now, Rivero!" Ray stood in the edge of the area, leaning on Dimitri for support.

The King of Shadows scowled at the sound of his real name. "You really haven't changed at all, Raymundo."

"I command you to surrender now."

"I don't take orders from you anymore!" He snapped. "How can you sleep at night knowing how many innocent lives you've taken?"

Ray raised his hands in surrender. "I don't. I can never forgive myself for what I've done and I'm not asking you to forgive me. This fight is between you and me, please, I'm begging you, leave Coraline out of this."

Cora picked up the antidote then closed in hoping this time she'd manage to inject it. She had him right where she wanted him. She carefully administered the antidote through his clothes. He didn't even flinch. She'd have no way of knowing if it worked until he tried to teleport again.

He placed a hand on his chin for a few moments. I'm sorry, but I'm afraid it's too late for that." Without hesitation Rivero's sword tore through Cora's abdomen and she collapsed onto the soaked ground.

Adrenaline rushed through her body, she needed to keep fighting. When she tried to get up pain surged through her entire body. She gasped for air despite how agonizing it was to do so. Her white T-shirt was completely stained red from her blood.

"Tell me Raymundo, how does it feel to watch the only person that gives a damn about you die right in front of your eyes?"

"BURN IN HELL!" Ray shouted between sobs. He fell onto his knees beside her. "Please stay with me Coraline I can't lose you." He gently whispered trying to control his tears.

"You're gonna pay for messing with my best friend!" Dimitri tightly gripped his sword.

The King of Shadows rolled his eyes. "Oh, please I've taken down men three times your size with twice your skill what makes you think you can defeat me."

"Maybe I can't defeat you," Dimitri gestured towards the entrance. "but I bet they can."

There stood Scarlet and Zyler followed by the entire pack of Tibicenas.

"You are going down," Zyler exclaimed.

"Imposible! They are loyal to me alone!"

The pack fiercely growled at the dark figure in front of them.

"Not anymore," Scarlet interjected. "You've hurt these animals and now they're going to hurt you back."

The pack circled Rivero with their teeth bared. For a brief moment fear flashed through his eyes. "You should fear me I am the most powerful magician who's ever lived." His voice cracked with anxiety. He tried to teleport, but nothing happened. He tried again to no avail. "How?"

Cora smirked. Nomatter what happens to her she was pleased to know she'd played a part in the King of Shadows demise.

The Tibicenas closed in on the King of Shadows then pounced on top of their prey. His loud cries echoed through the arena. After several moments Scarlet called the pack back to her.

Galen Rivero forced himself to his feet. He was able to stand despite being covered from head to toe in bites and scratches. "You didn't kill me." He laughed to himself.

"We aren't murderers like you." Cora said desperately trying not to lose consciousness, because she feared if she did she may she may never wake up.

"You're going to regret letting me live."

He was probably right, but Cora refused to stoop to his level. The ground was soaked with her blood. She was fading quickly and couldn't keep her eyes open for much longer.

Ray scooped her up in his arms. "Don't worry, Val is coming back with help, they should be here any minute now.

"I need you to promise me something." Cora croaked with what little life force she had left.

Ray nodded.

"No matter what happens, I need you to promise me you won't let it change you."

"I promise."

"Thank you." She placed a gentle kiss on his lips before everything faded to black.

21

EPILOGUE

The blonde was awoken by a familiar voice followed by a loud beeping sound.

"I always believed you'd be able to defeat the King of Shadows and I was right," her grandmother boasted.

Cora wondered if her ears deceived her. "But I wasn't really the one who defeated him technically it was Scarlet and the Tibicenas," She argued.

"Maybe the Tibicenas delivered the final blow, but everything was made possible by you,"

Cora raised an eyebrow in confusion.

"You're the one who brought all these people together. You're the one who inspires the people in your life to become someone better. Not to mention you tamed the Blood King. What I'm trying to say is I love you and I'm so proud of you."

She couldn't control the tears rolling down her cheeks somehow she knew this would the last time they ever spoke. "I love you too."

"It's time for you to go. They need you back."

Her sapphire eyes shot open. She was lying in a bed that wasn't her own. The steady beeping continued. Her body ached as she sat up. Her abdomen was wrapped in thick bandages, suddenly all the memories of the previous night came flooding back to her. She got stabbed! The steady beeping persisted to aggravate her. She realized the noise was coming from the heart beat monitor she was hooked up to. She glanced out the window and sure enough all of the dark clouds had cleared and all she could see was clear blue sky. She let out a long sigh hoping it would ease the pain.

A nurse popped into to the room and beamed when she realized Cora was awake. She proceeded to ask Cora a bunch of questions, most of which Cora answered to the best of her abilities even though she was still pretty out of it. Then the nurse ran out of the room and returned with her parents.

"What the hell were you thinking?" her mother exclaimed with teardrops in her eyes. "You could've been killed out there!"

Cora scoured through her mind looking for the right words to comfort her mother, but none came to her. "I'm sorry." Were the only words she managed to utter.

Her father tightly wrapped his arms around her. "I know I should be furious right now, but I'm just so happy you're alive," he whispered in her ear.

"What happened?" Cora asked wearily.

"You were stabbed!"

"What happened after that?"

"Your friend, I think her name was Val, called the authorities saying something about an evil wizard disguised as the prince," her father explained. "They assumed this was some kind of prank, but decided to send a few men down there just in case, and sure enough there he was. They saw him stab you from the far side of the arena, but couldn't stop him from hurting you in time. They brought you to the hospital and took him into custody."

"How long have I been unconscious?"

"They rushed you into surgery about six hours ago and you've been out since."

She let out a long yawn. This entire experience had exhausted her and right now all she wanted to do was fall fast asleep.

"Enough talk about that," her father tried to change the subject. "Do you want me to get you some tea?"

The thought of tea made her stomach churn. "No thanks, I'll have a hot chocolate, please."

After her parents left, she napped for the rest of the afternoon. She felt much better apart from the stabbing pain in her gut. She needed a distraction. She turned on the tv.

"This just in: DNA testing proves that our beloved Prince Lyon has been replaced by a look alike. The police have taken the perpetrator into custody for identity theft and violently attacking a young woman named Coraline Bowman. The victim is currently recovering at Clearview General Hospital.

Thessionia's finest warriors are searching for our lost prince. The question on everyone's mind is, what does this mean for the monarchy?"

That was an excellent question and one she didn't have an answer to. What would happen now? For some reason her heart broke just thinking about Price Lyon. She never knew him, not the real version of him anyway, but she still mourned the loss of him. She switched off the tv and rolled over trying to fall back to sleep.

A loud knock sounded from the door and Val, Zyler and Ray promptly entered the room.

"Hey," she said with what little the enthusiasm she could muster. It's not that she wasn't happy to have company, she was just flooded with emotions at the moment and didn't know how to cope with them.

"I thought you'd be more enthusiastic considering we just defeated the King of Shadows and all," Zyler pointed out.

Cora rubbed her eyes. "I'm tired, that's all."

"Perhaps these will make you feel better." Val handed her a box of chocolates. "I'm really sorry I didn't stay for the final fight. I didn't think I'd be of much use on the battlefield so I decided to go fetch the authorities instead."

"Don't apologize, I probably wouldn't have made it out alive if help arrived any later."

"I've got BIG news for you guys!" Zyler pulled a sheet of paper out of his pocket and proudly showed it off. "The Thesonian Guild Association heard about our work taking down the King of Shadows and they want to make us an official guild." Sure enough, the paperwork in his hands was legitimate.

Cora ran her fingers over the emblem stamped on the papers. "Are you serious?"

"Of course I'm serious!"

Cora forced a small smile.

"Are you not excited?" Val asked.

"I am excited, but I'm just kind of upset at the moment."

"What's wrong?" Ray asked. This was the first time he had spoken since he entered the room.

"The King of Shadows has taken so much away from everyone and so many people have died by his hands. I'm so unsure of what will happen next. Since Prince Lyon is dead there's no heir to the throne." Cora said defeatedly.

"Maybe he had a long lost relative or something." Zyler suggested.

Val quickly checked her phone. "Zyler and I have a meeting with the Prestige Program's science division about some new ideas I've been working on," She set the papers from the Guild Association down next to Cora. The top page contained the signatures of Scarlet, Val and Zyler. "If you decide to join all you have to do is sign here then turn these papers into the Thesonian Guild Association if not just give them back to me."

Cora nodded. "I'll think about it."

Zyler and Val said there goodbyes and then promptly left the hospital room leaving Ray and Cora alone.

Ray stood shyly in the corner of the room holding a stuffed lion with a big blue bow tied to it and a card that said. "Get well soon, Cora."

She pointed at the lion. "Is that for me?"

He nodded enthusiastically and hand it to her. "You're father said you like them."

"You talked to my dad?"

"He found out I've been living in your guest house. I told him that I didn't have anywhere to live so you said I could stay there and he said any friend of yours was a friend of his. We talked for a long time and he said I could stay as long as I was willing to do chores."

She hugged the stuffed lion tightly. "I love it! I'm gonna name him Ray Jr."

Ray chuckled. "If that makes you happy. Ray Jr. it is."

She rested her hand on top of his. "I'm happy to see you."

He kissed her forehead. "I'm happy to see you too and I want you to know no matter what happens I'll be here for you and protect you with my life, always and forever."

She squeezed his hand. "And I promise I'll always be by your side to comfort you and keep you sane when you feel like falling apart." She pulled him into a kiss that felt like, for a few minutes, it stopped time itself.

Milton Keynes UK
Ingram Content Group UK Ltd.
UKHW050637250923
429338UK00018B/950